MAX LAKEMAN AND THE BEAUTIFUL STRANGER

A NOVEL BY JON COHEN

WARNER BOOKS

A Warner Communications Company

Copyright © 1990 by Jon Cohen
All rights reserved.
Warner Books, Inc., 666 Fifth Avenue, New York, NY 10103

Printed in the United States of America
First Printing: March 1990
10 9 8 7 6 5 4 3 2 1

Library of Congress Cataloging-in-Publication Data

Cohen, Jon.
    Max Lakeman and the beautiful stranger / Jon Cohen.
        p.   cm.
    ISBN 0-446-51533-7
    I. Title.
PS3553.042433M3   1990
813'.54—dc20

                                                    89-39070
                                                    CIP

Book design: H. Roberts

For Mary

Mary Hasbrouck, Ruth Malone, Margaret Robinson,
Gail Hochman, Jamie Raab, Bloop and Hennig—
Thank you.

MAX LAKEMAN AND THE BEAUTIFUL STRANGER

Presentiment—is that long Shadow—on the Lawn—
Indicative that Suns go down—

The Notice to the startled Grass
That Darkness—is about to pass—

Emily Dickinson

1

*M*AX Lakeman, ever the alien, sat in his lawn chair in the thin shade of a dying peach tree, watching his family. Who were these creatures? How had they gotten into his backyard? What did they want?

One of the two smaller creatures turned and looked across the lawn at him. It had spotted him. Contact was imminent. It spoke, startling Max with its command of the Earthling language.

"Daddy. Come play."

Daddy?

"Max. Get the ketchup and relish, will you?" his wife, Nelly, called to him. "The burgers are about done."

Ketchup? Relish?

The two small creatures, Ben and Nora, stared at their daddy. Nelly stared, too. Max stared back at the three of them.

Had someone at that moment placed a bottle of ketchup and a jar of relish next to his wife and children and said to him, *Please tell us which two of these five items before you are not members of your immediate family*, Max would have had serious difficulty providing the correct answer.

But as it always did, the moment passed. Max rose stiffly, rubbing the red diagonals branded into the backs of his legs by the lawn chair. He waved to Nelly, as if to give her the all-clear signal. Hi honey, I'm back, his wave said. Didn't mean to scare you. I just stepped out for a minute, that's all. He smiled at his children. Daddy's okay. Really. It's safe now. You can go back to playing in the sandbox.

"Relish?" he called to Nelly. "Which kind do you want, Indian or sweet?" Wow her with details, Max. Show her you're right on top of things. "I'll get some mustard, too!"

Max hurried up the back steps and into the cool, dim kitchen. He leaned over the sink, turned on the faucet, and splashed water on his face. Then he looked out the window at his family. It was a family he recognized now. Nelly, Ben, and Nora. Sometimes he got a little distracted, that's all. Sometimes he wandered.

He settled down to the business at hand. He knelt before the open refrigerator and found the relishes, Indian and sweet. The ketchup, however, threw him off. There were three damn bottles and every one of them was opened. He hesitated before each bottle, wondering if it was possible to choose the wrong one. He reached out and of course got the bottle with the half-congealed red smear on the back. The wrong one.

The red, dribbling down between his thumb and forefinger, made him feel slightly queasy, as if he had just slashed himself with the paring knife. He did not like to get food slime on himself, especially slime so ominous in color and consistency. He held his hand far out in front of him, eyeing it nervously as he moved toward the sink.

Nelly, walking into the kitchen, caught the tail end of this performance—the outstretched hand smeared with ketchup, Max's mutterings as he worked the soap between his fingers. "Hey, Lady Macbeth," she said, "you doing all right in here?"

Max gave her a look over his shoulder as he washed. "How is it possible to have three opened bottles of ketchup in the refrigerator?"

"Uh-oh," said Nelly. "Please. Not the decadence lecture."

"It's beyond decadence."

"Oh, God," said Nelly, poking him in the back. "Not the beyond-decadence lecture."

He turned. "You're painful, you know that?"

"I can't help myself, Max. I go to the store, I see all that ketchup sitting there on the racks, and I gotta buy it. It's sick, I know, but I just can't get enough." She clutched his shirt and bugged her eyes.

Max waited patiently for her to finish being funny, then plucked her hands off his shirt. She straightened up and smiled.

"I forget," he said, trying not to smile back at her. "Why was it I married you?"

"Because you like ketchup?" she said in her sweet way.

Max ran over to the stove and reached for the spatula that resided in a greasy frying pan. "That's it!" he said. "I'm going to have to teach you a lesson." A piece of egg drooled off the end of the spatula.

Nelly backed away. "Not a . . . cooking lesson. Oh, please, not that."

He approached her slowly, slicing the air like a swordsman. He grinned evilly, raising one eyebrow. "You think you're so smart. Well, now I'm going to slice you. And dice you." It was an old game.

"No."

"Yes," he said, closing in.

"You can't."

"I can."

She reached behind her and grabbed a towel off the towel rack. She gave it a twirl and snapped it at him. "Hah. Back off, buster, or you'll lose body parts you didn't even know you had."

"That's a risk," he said, "I'm just going to have to take." He made a martial arts attack noise and lunged at her with the spatula. Nelly dodged around him and popped him a good one on the ass.

They danced back and forth, attacked and counterattacked, spatula against towel. Nelly was about to gain the upper hand when she saw Ben standing at the screen door. Max stopped midparry, letting the spatula slowly drop to his side.

Ben, as he so often did, looked bewildered. Max could see Ben's little brain rifling through his response index. Cry, laugh, run, wet pants?

"Playing," Nelly said, opening the screen door and kneeling down to him. "Mommy and Daddy were just playing." She hugged him, and Max saw Ben eyeing the spatula over Nelly's shoulder.

Well, there you go, thought Max. Add spatulas to the list of objects seared into Ben's subconscious, a benign item which from this moment on will elicit a complicated and twisted response. Twenty years from now, thousands of therapy dollars later, Ben will be a breakfast cripple, unable to use a spatula to flip an egg or toss a pancake. Every time he sees one he'll remember his father beating his mother in the kitchen while she defended herself pathetically with a dish towel.

But Ben had something else on his mind. "Nora," he said, suddenly smiling, happy to betray his younger sister. "She's eating the buns."

Nora! Max shot past Nelly and Ben. Christ, Nora alone in the backyard, helpless amidst the barbecue grill, the plastic wrappers, the knives and forks, the glass bottles.

When Max reached her, Nora was sitting in the grass mangling her third hamburger bun. She was not eating them, as Ben had been so quick to report, but simply pulling them apart and throwing the pieces into the air. Max stopped behind her, breathless, sweaty, and exceedingly grateful.

How fraught with peril, this child business. Every stage of it, fraught, fraught, fraught. Max remembered the woozy feeling of excitement when Nelly had revealed her pregnancy to him, the pregnancy that would result in Ben.

As elated as he was, a little phrase kept popping into his

mind: Now I've done it, now I've done it, I've really done it this time.

Pregnancy threw him. It just didn't seem possible—a human being growing inside another human being. Max imagined one of those wooden toys: you open one and there's another, open that one and out pops another, on and on.

He asked Nelly crazy late-night questions no ordinary woman would have tolerated. But Nelly knew Max.

"Um, Nelly," he said, lightly tracing his finger along the side of her ripe belly. It was late, she had almost been asleep.

"Won't be long now, huh?" he said.

"Two weeks," she mumbled. She reached for his finger. "That's too tickly."

"It's definitely a nine-month thing, right?"

"Right."

There was a silence, and then he said, "It wouldn't keep going or anything, you wouldn't just keep getting bigger, right?"

"Right." Nelly smiled in the dark beside him. "Unless I had one of them teenage pregnancies. You know, pregnant for fifteen years, then give birth to a teenager." She laughed and went to sleep. Max had feverish dreams of watching the Macy's Thanksgiving parade on TV, and right behind the huge balloons of Underdog and Bullwinkle would come a blimplike Nelly, tethered and floating high above the crowd.

Max looked down at Nora surrounded by ravaged hamburger buns. When she had tossed the pieces into the air, what had she been imagining? Flowers dropping gently, a shower of stars? Certainly she hadn't done it just to watch the flight patterns of hunks of bun.

Max rescued the rest of the buns and scooped up his young daughter. He pushed his face close to hers. "Nora, you mustn't do that. That's food. Food is for eating." He tried not to smile as he said all this. He was a terrible disciplinarian. In later years, his children would walk all over him, he knew.

Nelly and Ben approached. "Doesn't she get punished?" he said, a look of disappointment on his sweet face.

"I've taken care of it, thank you, Ben." Maybe Ben should be the family enforcer. He had a keener sense of justice than did Max. Max reached out his hand, but Ben declined to take it. Oh, Ben, Ben, thought Max, forgive your father for being so weak.

A faded garnet Chevy station wagon with fake wood siding pulled into the driveway and honked. Emmett and Doris Lakeman, Max's parents, had at last arrived.

"They're here," Max and Nelly said simultaneously, then looked at each other. Max shrugged and placed his squirming Nora on the grass.

"They're here!" Ben said, emitting an enthusiasm his parents could not muster.

"We're here!" said Doris Lakeman, poking her head out of the window and waving. Emmett honked the horn again. When he was in that old station wagon, he let his horn do the talking. He had a whole honking language, a vocabulary of longs and shorts, louds and softs, from his quick jaunty honk of greeting, to a screaming, outraged, blast-them-the-god-damn-hell-off-the-road honk. Nelly called him Herr Honk-meister.

Emmett got out of the car, walked around it, and opened the door for his wife. Nelly teased Max about this when the two of them drove someplace. She'd wait on the passenger side after Max got out, and say, "O son of Honkmeister, aren't you going to open the door for your Honkfrau?"

"You're late," Max called to them. "We were about to eat without you." He watched the two of them approach. Were these creatures really his parents? The alien aura was creeping over him again. He was on a distant planet visiting a galactic zoo, and in the large homey cage marked EARTH: HOMO SAPIENS stood Emmett and Doris Lakeman, prime examples of the species.

Emmett was six foot two. Max knew this because Emmett's height was marked in heavy pencil on his parents' bath-room door. Below that dark mark was a series of other pencil lines—Max's recorded growth. The lines stopped short at five foot ten, there for all the world to see. Emmett was six-two, bushy of eyebrow, and except for a thin half ring of coarse white hair, bald as a potato. His face had a look of perpetual astonishment, probably because he was a bit pop-eyed. He wore glasses, the only ones Max ever knew him to wear. They were made of pale, yellowed plastic and were held together at the right corner by a dingy wad of tape. That knobby, wadded corner was like the swollen knuckle of an aging, ar-thritic hand. Or maybe, Max sometimes imagined, it was a third eyeball Emmett kept under wraps as a spare. It was big enough.

Emmett always wore a hat or a cap of some kind, a hold-over from his days as a railroad conductor. The hats came off only when circumstances called for a switch to another sort of hat—the green felt house hat came off for the Phillies cap Emmett wore for driving, and the Phillies cap would be re-placed by the white safari helmet he wore for working in the yard. Max had given the safari helmet to Emmett as a joke and was mortified when Emmett actually took to it. Nelly claimed that Emmett had a secret hat he wore only when he went to the bathroom, and another when he made love to Doris. Max cringed at these speculations because they rang true.

Emmett looked down at his wristwatch as he walked across the lawn with Doris. He was shaking his head in ex-asperation. It killed him to be late, the ultimate failure for a railroad conductor, even a retired one. Max was glad he had not been in the car with him on the way over. He could just see Doris bracing her arm against the dashboard as Emmett shot through yellow lights and floored it through stop signs. When Max was little, he used to sit in Emmett's lap and lean his ear against his father's big chest, and instead of a heartbeat he was sure he could hear the muffled tick of a clock.

"Welcome. You're not at all late," said Nelly. She was good to Emmett. "Come on over here and sit in the shade. Ben, pull that chair over here for your grandmother."

Doris came up to Max. Max, as he always did, checked out the mole on the side of her neck. He was sure that the mole once had strong, distinct boundary lines like Nevada or New Mexico. Over the last few months, though, the sides had begun to shift and soften, to take on more of a Maine or West Virginia look. When the thing became Hawaii, Max was sure his mother would be a goner.

But Doris struck first. "You look thin," she said, touching his cheek with the back of her hand, and squinting at him.

"Mom, I *am* thin. Your son is an ectomorph."

"No, Smarty. I mean unhealthy thin."

"I weigh one hundred and forty-seven pounds. It's what I've weighed since high school."

"Well, you're not *in* high school now. You should weigh more."

Max pointed to the side of her neck, countering her. "Since we're discussing health issues here, when's the last time you had that mole checked out?"

Doris looked away, covering the spot with her hand. "That's a beauty mark, not a mole."

"I tell her the same thing, same thing," Emmett chimed in. " 'Go to the doctor, get it looked at.' Does she do it? No."

Ben went up to his grandmother and wrapped himself around her leg. "Well, at least someone loves me," she said.

"We all love you," said Nelly.

"Right," said Emmett. "Everybody loves everybody, so get your mole checked." He sat down. "Now let's eat."

"Right," Max said. "Nelly, come help me with the burgers."

They watched as Nora and Ben climbed all over Doris. Emmett sat at the table in front of his paper plate waiting for his burger. He liked the grandchildren all right, but he was not so big on the physical stuff. Let Doris handle that. Doris was the family love machine.

"You look thin," Nelly whispered to Max, smiling.

"Say, haven't I heard that somewhere before?" He flipped a hamburger on to the plate she held out for him, and rolled his eyes. "You know, I'm thinking of having some tests run to see if I'm really a Lakeman."

"Oh, you're a Lakeman. There's definitely a bit of Herr Honkmeister and Doris in you."

"You think so?"

But he supposed it was true. Max was slender, like his father, but not so tall. His hair was curly, like Doris's, a feature that struck suddenly at the onset of puberty. He could recall the exact moment the curls had come. It was after football practice in seventh grade. He entered the locker room, took off his helmet, and *bam*, there they were, as if the helmet had actually been one of those hair driers in a beauty salon and thirteen-year-old Max had told the hairdresser he wanted a totally new look. He certainly got it. From straight to curly in the course of one football practice. It was very traumatic. He spent the early part of adolescence trying to straighten his ridiculous hair with stolen globs of his mother's Dippity-Doo hair gel. In looks he was definitely a Lakeman. He sighed.

They brought the hamburgers back to the table, and Emmett took two and buried them beneath a precarious mountain of pickles, onions, and mustard. His jaws opened to a point just short of actual dislocation. Doris, in contrast to her voracious husband, took half a burger, no bun at all, and embellished it with a tiny dollop of ketchup.

Nelly set up Nora, and Max took care of Ben, who offered detailed instructions on how his father was to prepare his meal. Daddy created a small crisis when he put the mustard in the wrong place.

At last, with his little tribe under control for the moment, Max stood up to fetch his own hamburger from the grill. As he stood a few feet apart, watching them closely, he smiled to himself and thought, Max Lakeman, this is your family. How in heaven's name had he ever come by them?

By staying put. Max had always assumed that he was not destined for great things or faraway places. He was tethered, by his need for connection and familiarity, to his hometown of Gramenton, outside of Philadelphia. The itchy words and hot longings of his high school classmates made no sense to him. Why were they so crazy to get out of Gramenton?

Max liked to walk the streets and look at the houses, the trees and lawns. It was a beautiful place, but it was not only that. Because he had lived in Gramenton for over thirty years, there were particular lawns, particular trees or houses with which he had old associations: trees he had climbed, lawns he had cut through to get to secret places, houses he had stood patiently in front of waiting for friends to come out. The past was all around him, fused with the present. Some mornings Max would kiss his wife good-bye, walk out of his house, and for a moment not know what year it was, who he might find—maybe a childhood friend with whom he could play kickball?

By not leaving Gramenton, not joining in the great exodus of his high school classmates bound for glory in Tulsa, St. Louis, or wherever they ended up, Max managed to marry a hometown girl, Nelly MacKinnon. It was, he believed, the great achievement of his life. How had he ever gotten her to agree to such a thing?

In fact, Nelly married Max because he was a nice guy. She was very practical. Max was not a wildly exciting man. But he was comforting. She knew he would be good to a wife and children. She knew, in the larger sense, that he would always be there for her. And if he was odd, if there were moments where he revealed a distinctly alien nature, she forgave him that. Nelly liked Max, and she loved him for being so likeable.

Sometimes, lying next to her at night, Max would sneak peeks at Nelly. He couldn't believe it, couldn't believe he coaxed this wonderful creature into marrying him. Actually, he didn't have to coax her at all. She was the one who suggested they take the plunge.

"You mean get married?" he had said.

"You bet," she said, wrapping her arms around him one soft summer night.

"Wow."

"Pretty big stuff, huh?" said Nelly.

"I thought only parents were allowed to get married," Max said.

Max loved being married to Nelly, the whole day-after-day package. From good morning until good night, he reveled in the incessant contact, the ordinary business of living with a wife. See the woman next to me, the one with the beautiful brown braid and luscious white skin, he sometimes wanted to say in supermarkets or malls, well, she's my wife. Can you believe it?

Of course Max and Nelly had their moments. Nothing dangerous, nothing that threatened the marital infrastructure. The little things sometimes annoyed, like Max's insistence on watching all three network news programs simultaneously, or at least as simultaneously as button pushing on the remote control would allow. Like Nelly's aggressive morning cheerfulness in the face of Max's inability to evolve beyond the Neanderthal stage for the first half hour after rising from bed. Little things.

Not only was he allowed to get married, Max soon discovered, but he was also allowed to have children. Having children was not easy for Max, not that it was especially easy for Nelly.

Ben, now five, came first. Max remembered those nine months as if he was the one carrying fetal Ben around in his own belly. When Nelly began to gain weight, so did he. Morning sickness, aching back, tired legs—all of it, Max matched Nelly symptom for symptom. His imagination was as fertile as Nelly's womb. When she finally broke water and went into labor, Nelly said to him, smiling, "Guess this is where we separate the men from the boys." Actually, Max thought he felt a little contraction or two, but he said nothing.

The birth of Ben was a relatively easy event compared to Nora's entrance into the world, she the destroyer of hamburger buns, now age two. Nora was a great source of anxiety and guilt for Max because she turned out to be a prenatal lingerer. Come nine months, Nora declined to be born, content to remain in her own amniotic Jacuzzi. So at nine months, ten days, the doctors had to go in after her.

Nelly under the knife. As the doctors explained this to him, Max could barely hear or understand them because the little phrase that had accompanied the birth of Ben had popped into his head again: Now I've done it, now I've done it, I've really done it this time. Only now it was worse: during the course of Nelly's cesarean, Max lapsed into a mental state that he had come to call the Church of the Scary Jesus Christ.

The Church of the Scary Jesus Christ was a place in Max's sometimes fevered mind, a room he sent himself to when he was full of guilt or fear. At that moment he felt good and guilty for being the ultimate cause of Nelly's cesarean. Plus he was scared absolutely spitless. The room, as Max imagined it, was dimly lit, perhaps by a single bare red or yellow bulb. Beneath the swinging bulb Max saw himself sitting, a penitent figure cramped beneath a small wooden desk, a desk that might have been pilfered from an elementary school of the late 1950s. On the smeared gray wall before him hung endless crass depictions of Christ on the cross—the wounds hideous with impossible quantities of bright red blood dripping from them, the bodies waxy green and skeletal, the agonized eyes rolling toward heaven. And all the Christs would suddenly turn their crowned, lacerated heads and whisper to Max in hoarse unison, *Join us, join us.*

Thankfully, he did not have to attend a long service at

the Church of the Scary Jesus Christ. The cesarean turned out to be quick and routine, Nora issuing forth without incident, though somewhat crankily. Max took longer to recover, secretly fingering his psychic wounds and hearing faint whispers, *Join us, join us*, each time he viewed Nelly's healing scar.

To feed, clothe, and in general provide for their burgeoning brood, Max mowed lawns, and Nelly worked as a registered nurse at a nearby community hospital. That Max should still be mowing lawns, a job he had had since junior high school, would seem amusing, pathetic, to his old classmates who were making it big in Tulsa and St. Louis. They would certainly not believe an even more astonishing fact—that he loved his work.

Max was that rarity who could not imagine doing anything else. He wasn't dumb, he wasn't a misfit or a loser. He simply took great pleasure in cutting grass. Extreme pleasure. The smell of new mown grass spiced with a whiff of gasoline delighted him. The sound of his exquisitely tuned mowers was muted music to his earmuff-protected ears. Also, he liked to be alone, unencumbered by either boss or underling. Alone, walking up and down his lawns beneath the big old trees of Gramenton.

Sometimes, lulled by the sound of his mowers and the warmth of a summer day, Max would enter into a kind of trance, a dream. He'd look up and find that everything around him had disappeared, even the mower he was pushing was gone, and he'd be alone on a great green lawn, a perfect sea of green. It was a very happy little moment, it was where he wanted to be, without Nelly or Ben or Nora, just all by himself on that endless lawn.

He'd told Nelly about it once and of course instantly panicked her.

"You mean, you're going along behind an incredibly lethal machine and you just fade out?"

He should never have mentioned it. "No, it's not like that exactly."

But she wasn't hearing him. "That's great. That's just great. One of these times you're going to come out of one of your little trances and find your severed toes flying across the lawn."

Max never brought it up again.

In the fall he raked yards, in the winter he cleared snow with a plow attachment he put on the front of his pickup. He did a bit of this and that during the off-season, but it was the mowing of summer lawns, in and out of the shade, that he truly loved.

Nelly, of course, was far more matter-of-fact about her career. She had few transcendent moments of joy like Max, moving amidst the sun and shade. That's because in nursing there was a great deal to bring you to your senses, like pain, blood, death, and mucus. Nelly was very conversant in these unsavory matters, even if Max rarely let her converse.

"Don't tell me!" he'd say, when Nelly began to tell him about her day.

"Oh, Max, I have to. Even I, the hardened professional, was grossed out by this patient."

"Nelly, for God's sake, if you're grossed out, you know I'll be. Why do you do this?" Of course, a part of Max secretly wanted the gory details.

Whether he wanted them or not Nelly was going to give them to him. "This guy had this hole, I mean, you could have parked your pickup in this thing, this major hole right under his—"

"Aaah," Max cried, covering his ears and stomping his feet. He'd learned the move from watching one of Ben's tantrums.

Nelly waited. "You done now? He had this hideous, pus-filled hole . . ."

Nelly believed in educating the general public, including Max, about the unpretty side of life. She was big on administering doses of reality.

* * *

There was one other member of Max's immediate family. Bilko, the dog.

When Max was filling out some kind of health or insurance form and there was a space for "significant other" or whom to notify in the "event of death," he was tempted to put down "Bilko." Bilko was female, about eight years old, and of a mix of breed that suggested her mother had been indiscreet. She had short, uninteresting grayish hair, a pink and black nose, a small head, and a left ear that seemed smaller than the right.

She appeared eight years before, quite literally out of the blue. Max had finished his last lawn of the day, and since the owners were not home, he plopped down on the freshly cut grass and lay contentedly staring up at the blue sky. Several minutes into his reverie, something pink and black entered the edge of his line of vision. Max twisted his head around, and there before him stood young (and as yet unnamed) Bilko, with no collar and no owner in sight. A gift from the gods!

Max was a lover of dogs the way some men are indiscriminate lovers of women. Nothing turned his head more quickly than a dog trotting down the street or cutting through a backyard. Dogs could do no wrong; no amount of garbaging, rug pissing, or flea infestation could alter the course of Max's true love. Bilko, in all other eyes save Max's, was unremarkable. She knew no tricks, had few endearing habits, but he didn't care.

Sometimes Max talked to Bilko when he thought no one was listening, as he had the other morning when he was overheard by an amused Nelly.

Max was on the front porch scratching Bilko's ears when suddenly something rustled in the azaleas across the street. Bilko turned to Max, and he nodded.

"I heard it too, Bilko."

They both stared again at the azaleas.

"I dunno, Bilko, I dunno. . . ."

Another rustle. Bilko got to her feet.

"Think we're talking squirrel, here, Bilko. I think we're talking serious squirrel, maybe two or three. A squirrel fiesta."

Bilko started to growl, and Max growled with her, getting her psyched for the attack.

"A squirrel convention, that's what it is! You got to break it up, Bilko, you got to go over there and bust them squirrels, bring some law and order to this street."

And Bilko lunged across the street, barking and yapping and carrying on, giving the squirrels ample warning, plenty of time to scramble, because she didn't actually want to risk catching one. Too dangerous.

"Good girl," Max shouted. "That'll teach 'em, huh?" as Bilko trotted triumphantly back to him, while Nelly watched from a distance, shaking her head and smiling.

Emmett pushed back from the picnic table, replete after two hamburgers and a hot dog. There was a splotch of mustard on the right side of his mouth.

Max touched the right side of his own mouth and said to him, "You gonna get that, or are you saving it for later?" It was a line Emmett had used often when Max was small.

Emmett raised one eyebrow, then wiped the mustard off with his finger, licked it, and said, "I'm not the only slob here. You got a hunk of relish on your cheek, Bub." He smiled triumphantly.

Doris piped in, "I'm surprised you two don't have more on your faces the way you rush with your food."

"Thin as I am, you don't want me to eat?" Max said.

"You need to slow down, is all I'm saying," said Doris. "Slow down, set an example for your children."

Ah, the children. Was it at all possible to influence them, to shape their little psyches? The evidence did not seem to support it. Ben, with Nora in rapt attention, was holding his charred hot dog in his fist, using the end of it to create ketchup and mustard paintings on his paper plate. It looked like fun.

A light breeze kicked up, and Emmett lifted his hat, leaned into it a moment, then put the hat back in place. "You figured out what you're doing about vacation? Summer's slipping away, you know."

Summer's slipping away. Expressions like that unnerved Max. A while back he had been standing in line behind two women in a drugstore. They were chatting, Max listening in as always, and the short woman with blue-gray hair suddenly sighed, put her hand on her friend's arm, and said, "Don't de days get by." Max felt a little dizzy and drifted away to the personal hygiene section until the two women left. He did not like reminders of how fast it was all going.

Doris said, "Max, you remember our big car trip out west when you and Fred were small? Nelly, you should do that, has Max ever told you what fun that was?"

"He has," said Nelly. "And he's showed me pictures of it, too." Pictures of two scrawny, hot, and miserable boys, a hot and harried mother, and a hot and angry father. It sure looked like fun.

The car trip out west, Max thought, the true test of the American Family. If ever there was a chamber of tortures, it was that 1964 Chevy station wagon, jam packed with the essentials of modern travel, the textured plastic of the car seat like sitting on a waffle iron, the sweltering wind bringing to the back of the car, where Max lay cramped and miserable with his brother, Fred, the smell of the burning highway and the dry foreign land whizzing past him.

Max could barely remember the Grand Canyon, Carlsbad Caverns, the Meteor Crater in Winslow, Arizona. But the athlete's foot, that he remembered! It began when the trip began, practically when they pulled out of the driveway in Gramenton. Just a tiny dry itchy spot on the middle toe of his right foot. The days passed, the Chevy surged across the great land, and bored and cramped Max picked and scratched at his toe. Then, along about east Texas, he discovered the ultimate toe scratching surface—the car upholstery with its deliciously raspy weave. From there on in, Max rubbed his toe back and forth like a madman. The patch of athlete's foot, which had up until that point been reasonably localized, now spread in red oozy trails across his foot. Max, though panicked, could not stop rubbing his inflamed appendage on the upholstery. Emmett and Doris knew nothing of this until they had reached San Luis Obispo, California, and Max was noticeably limping. Shame, mortification, and horror. Emmett took his lunkhead of a son to a clinic, and Max spent the remainder of the trip applying ointments to his ravaged foot.

Max looked down at his toe—the nail was twisted and nasty, a souvenir from that car trip of long ago.

"I don't know, maybe we'll go to the beach," he said. "I'm not really up for going anywhere big this summer."

"Are you ever?" said Nelly. "He never wants to leave his front yard."

"I don't know where he gets that from," said Doris. "Emmett and I are such great travelers."

True enough: Mexico, Jamaica, Europe. The whole bit. But that was not for Max. Occasionally he liked to venture forth and take in some strange terrain. The front yard, though, and the back, held a lot of appeal for Max. Sitting outside beneath his dying peach tree in the full and luscious presence of summer, his hand on Bilko's warm head, Nelly reading beside him, the children safely within view.

"We should travel home is where we should travel. It'll be dark soon," said Emmett.

"Don't you want to stay for the fireflies?" said Ben. Last week when his grandpa was over, they walked around the yard, Ben catching fireflies and putting them in Emmett's cupped hand. They'd get a lot, then Emmett would let them go, and Ben would stare as the cloud of insects floated up, shimmering into the night sky. Sometimes Max would watch his father watching the fireflies. Emmett's eyes seemed to catch some of the fireflies' glow, if only for a moment. It was in those moments Max knew he was Emmett Lakeman's son.

"We'll do the fireflies again next time," Emmett promised Ben.

Max walked them to the car.

"Stop by soon," said Doris. "The tomatoes are ripening up."

"I will," said Max. Tomato season, nothing like it. Grilled cheese and tomato, marinated tomatoes, BLT's.

"Well, good night, son," said Emmett.

The taillights disappeared around the corner, and Max gulped a little. He had had that old urge, when they had gotten in their car to head home, to hop in and go with them. As ridiculous as they sometimes were, he wanted to hop in, with his brother in the backseat beside him, and Emmett at the wheel driving them all home, home.

He stood a minute, then went back to help Nelly with the children. Nora was in her playpen out cold, and Ben was lolling in his mother's lap, fading fast.

"Which one do you want me to take?" asked Max.

"Take me," said drowsy Ben.

It all happened so fast with children, their little engines going full tilt one minute, then overheating and burning out the next.

Max scooped him up.

"I'm going to clean up this stuff, then I'll be up with the other limp one," said Nelly.

Too bad that children didn't have a button you could press to induce this wonderfully handy limp condition. Long car rides, trips to the supermarket, push that button and good-bye tears and tantrums.

Max opened the screen door with his foot and carried his son inside. He weaved through the darkened kitchen with his precious load, then hit the light at the bottom of the stairs with his elbow. Ben scrunched his eyes, sighed, and weakly brought his hands to his face. There was a spot where his T-shirt pulled up, revealing his soft belly, and Max lowered his head to kiss it.

"Don't," said Ben, and put his hand on his father's head to push it away. But sleep caught him and his fingers stayed there, loosely clutching one of Max's curls.

Nelly came in a few minutes later with Nora and, after wiping her tiny face and hands with a washcloth, put her in her crib and pulled a sheet up around her. When Nelly came into the hallway, Max came behind her and put his arms around her and touched one of her breasts with the back of his hand.

"Ah, my ample Aphrodite," he said.

"Uh-oh, here we go," said Nelly.

"Ah, my nicely knockered Nelly."

She pushed him away. "If you want some action, you better stick with the goddesses."

"Ah, let me see now. Ah, my voluptuous Venus," said Max. "How's that?"

"I knew you'd bring your Venus into it. Men are always bringing their Venuses into it."

"Well, I'd certainly like to try," said Max, nuzzling his nose into the back of her neck.

She turned and smiled a radiant smile that Venus herself might envy.

The moment was interrupted by a series of sharp barks.

"Bilko," said Max.

"Bilko can wait," said Nelly, giving him a midseduction-type kiss that involved some sort of complicated lip sucking. If Max wasn't in the mood, it made him feel geechy.

"I know that bark," said Max, pulling away. His lip felt numb where she had worked on it. "That bark is her 'I'm not stopping unless you come out here and forcibly restrain me' bark."

"Christ," said Nelly. "You get me all worked up with your Venus talk, then you're going to leave me like this?"

Bilko let loose with three sharp barks and a howl.

"Gotta go," said Max. "That's her heavy invasion bark."

"Like an alien starship fleet in the backyard?"

"Possibly, possibly. Or worse, the Drake's Irish setter taking a leak on our pachysandra."

"God forbid."

"Well, you have to look at it from Bilko's viewpoint."

"Don't I always?" said Nelly.

"Ooh. Jealous of a mere canine, are we?"

"*Mere* canine? Better keep your voice down, she might hear you."

"You're right, she's easily hurt."

"Unlike me, huh?"

"Now, now. Just let me get the damned dog before she wakes up the neighborhood, and I'll be right back."

Max winked hugely at her, then ran downstairs and out the back door to nab his evil hound. He could see her at the far end of the backyard, running back and forth.

"Bilko, come on, get your rat ass over here."

She barked again, three shorts and a long.

"Get over here, dog face, or you're in unbelievable trouble."

Bilko ran up to him, yapped, then ran back to the end of the yard where the rhododendrons grew tall and spooky. Max was afraid of the dark. He attributed this to the combination of having spent every Saturday of his childhood watching double-feature monster matinees and having poor vision. His poor eyesight would transform the objects in his childhood bedroom into the nightmare landscape of the movies—the radiator became a hunchback, his desk lamp a vulture, the chair a crouching vampire. He was constantly turning on his light or putting on his glasses to check things out.

"Bilko, please come here," he wheedled. A grown man afraid of the dark.

Something large appeared between the rustling leaves of

the rhododendrons. Bilko stopped midbark and growled. A sour taste came up from the back of Max's throat, and he tried to swallow it back down. This was precisely the kind of encounter he had spent his life desperately trying to avoid.

Bilko, in a spontaneous set of moves Max had never seen before, suddenly did two things—she sat on her haunches and went up into a beg, then dropped down and rolled over twice like a circus dog. It was not a good sign.

The wind picked up, and for a moment he thought he was on a tropical beach, so lush was the smell that reached him. A warm ocean, exotic flowers, unimaginable fruits. And then, before he could really focus or comprehend, out from the quivering leaves of the rhododendron stepped a beautiful woman in a white diaphanous robe—who pushed her full lips out at him across the distance in a kiss, who drew her white hand through her thick auburn hair, then held her hand out to him, who looked at him with soft eyes, and who suddenly vanished—all in four skips of Max's rapidly beating heart.

2

TWELVE hours later and thirteen miles away at Forkton Community Hospital, Nelly's heart, too, was skipping along at a hasty rate. It was the heartbeat of a nurse whose amazingly bad day was about to get worse. Three hours into her shift she still had baths to do, morning meds to give, an IV to restart because Mr. Ames in bed 14 had yanked his out, though he was in full restraints (he must have used his teeth), and now ("Be still my heart," Nelly whispered to herself) the charge nurse told her she was getting an admission from the ER. A gork. Forkton was living up to the nickname the nurses had given it—Gorktown. A Gorktown gork, some poor old guy the paramedics found dead in his bathroom, so they did him the favor of reviving him, sort of, and bringing him to the hospital where he could linger on a respirator and have numerous large tubes painfully inserted into small orifices. The only way to go, thought Nelly.

Other nurses would have lost it, would have shed tears in the bathroom or gone catatonic with overload and stood helplessly in the center of the nurse's station. Nelly considered those options briefly, taking in the chaos around her, the lab techs running, the doctors yelling, the patients groaning, then looked into the eyes of Rita, the large charge nurse. "I believe I have chosen the wrong occupation," said Nelly.

The charge nurse looked back at her, waiting.

"I believe," said Nelly, "this is all a cruel, cruel joke."

Waiting, the charge nurse waiting.

"And I believe," said Nelly, "that if I take this ER admission, you will owe me one."

"Nelly," said the charge nurse breaking into a huge grin that revealed cigarette-stained teeth, "I will definitely owe you one. If another gork comes into the ER, I'll either stall him till the next shift or turf him to another floor."

"You're swell, Rita."

"That's what they say," she laughed, pushing her large self between two arguing interns and disappearing into the confusion.

Nelly took a breath, licked her lips, and shifted her gears into high efficiency. The day, she swore, was not going to get away from her. She went in to Mr. Ames's room to start his IV before her admission came. Mr. Ames was a tad out of it, hence the wrist restraints.

"How you doing, Mr. Ames?" said Nelly. She was good to her patients even when she was rushed and they were unceasingly troublesome. Yesterday, unrestrained, Mr. Ames had pulled his feeding tube from his nose and emptied his urinal into the drawer of his bedside table. Better there than in his freshly made bed, had been Nelly's practical thought.

"I'm doing how I'm doing is how I'm doing," he replied, eyeing her warily.

Nelly smiled; she loved that kind of response. "Okay," she said, uncoiling her IV tubing.

"Who are you, the TV girl? My TV's on the fritz."

There was no TV in Mr. Ames's room. There were two ways to go about this. She could attempt to orient him to reality, by patiently explaining that she was a nurse here to start an IV. Of course, that would no doubt agitate him, and she would probably have to fight him all the way. Or she could go the TV girl route and see where it led.

"Yep," said Nelly, "that's me. What's the matter with your TV?"

"Reception!" shouted Mr. Ames. "Sound!" He struggled with his restraints.

"Easy, Mr. Ames, come on now," she said, gently placing her hand on his arm. "Tell you what, sounds like the antenna to me. We've been having all kinds of problems with the antennas on these sets. So I brought you a replacement," she said, holding up the IV tubing in front of him.

"Thatta girl," said Mr. Ames.

"Now this is a special kind of antenna, goes in your arm." She had reached the tricky part.

"My arm? You sure?"

"That's where they're putting them, these days."

"Well, if it'll help bring in 'The Andy Griffith Show,' I don't care if you stick the damn thing up my ass."

Nelly stuck the IV in his arm, and Mr. Ames was as good as gold.

"Girl, it's a miracle," Mr. Ames said when she finished. "I can see Andy and Goober clear as day."

Another satisfied customer, Nelly thought, leaving the room with a big smile on her face, her heart beating just fine.

Back in Gramenton, Max, as a man who had encountered a beautiful woman in the twilight rhododendrons might, was thinking about seeing things. Max had grown up seeing things. It all began, he believed, with his troublesome eyes. The eyes he got from Doris, surpassing even her great myopia. At four he was already wearing little Coke-bottle lenses. As a child, Max truly lived in two realities, and only a myopic could really understand this. There was the daytime glasses-on reality where everything was nice and normal and recognizable, and there was the reality of bedtime and glasses-off. Each object in his little room next to Fred's became something entirely different in Max's frightening nighttime world. While it was not comforting to know that he had a room filled with hunchbacks, vultures, and mummies, he had eventually come to accept it. After all, he was never actually attacked, eaten, or even mildly threatened. He figured, as the years passed, that his room must be some sort of monster way station, a rest stop they used between periods of wreaking havoc elsewhere.

So it was not outside the realm of possibility, in Max's myopic view, that a beautiful woman should be lurking in the rhododendrons. As a child at least, he had certainly seen more startling apparitions.

But (and the "but" was what dried the lining of Max's mouth and tightened his scrotum as he walked back and forth during his first lawn job the next day) he had had his glasses firmly on his nose, so it couldn't have been a vision thing. "But" number two: it had been, however, dark, and he was standing some distance away. And there were three beers in him. "But" number three: Bilko was present and definitely a participant in the event. That morning Max tried to get Bilko to beg, to roll over, anything, but she would have none of it. The scathing look she gave him clearly indicated her feelings about performing for human beings. Why, then, had she cavorted so readily last night?

And why, moving from "but"s to "why"s, hadn't he been a good boy and told his wife? After his heart had returned to its normal rate and rhythm, after he could breathe without wheezing and move his weakened legs again, he sneaked back into the house and slipped into bed while Nelly was in the bathroom. He had his eyes closed and the sheet up around him when she came into the bedroom.

Nelly regarded her husband a moment, then spoke. "Our mood changed, has it?"

Boy, had it. Max opened one eye, then closed it again.

"Men," said Nelly. "One minute they wanna, the next minute they don't wanna. What's a housewife to do?"

"Nelly," Max said, eyes closed, and voice a little squeaky from his rhododendron episode, "it's not that I don't want to."

"I know," she said. "It's not that you don't want to, it's just that you don't want to. Right?"

"Um, right," said Max.

"Okeydoke. But you will at least have to give me one good kiss."

Max sat up in bed and opened his arms to her. Now, now, now.

Tell her about the woman in the bushes *now*.

But he did not. Or he could not. The words, just waiting to leap out of his mouth, would not come. What was holding him back? Afraid Nelly might think he was crazy? No, Nelly knew he was crazy.

And then, with Nelly in his arms, a thought came to him. A rather disconcerting thought it was, too. He didn't want to say anything about the beautiful woman because talking about her would be betraying her. Then the next thought. Not talking about her was betraying Nelly.

And so it went—tell, not tell—until the sound of Nelly breathing evenly in her sleep reached his ears, and the decision was made for him.

Lawn-mowing therapy, nothing like it. By the fourth lawn, Max's encounter of the night before began to fade, crowded out by ordinary thoughts. What a fine summer day it was. He sat down on the curb when he was finished mowing and looked up and down the street. Sitting on the curb taking in the street was something he had once done a lot of.

There'd be four or five of them, and they'd all have their shirts off—being allowed to take your shirt off because it was now warm enough in the opinion of Doris and the other mothers. Summer began when the shirts came off. And then just sitting on the curb fiddling around with stuff in the gutter—old acorns, worms, bottle caps, trashy bits. That street, the physical street, had qualities that differentiated it from other streets in other neighborhoods. You used that raised hunk there for first base; the stretch down by the Gaffney's was flat and good for four square; the gooey spot beneath the second streetlight was where you'd pick tar bubbles when the hot sun softened the asphalt. Max hoped Ben and Nora would have such pleasures.

A car honked as it drove by him. Pete Folger, one of Max's old shirts-off-on-the-curb friends. Pete and Max had little to say to one another now; they were always just waving or hitting their horns in greeting. Max wondered if Pete remembered those days. But it pained Max even to be near him now, let alone talk to him. Pete had one of those panicky-looking faces that came from having married too soon, then kids too soon, too soon you-name-it. Disappointed people made Max anxious. He didn't like to know that men in households throughout the world were asking the big scary question, "Is this all there is?"

Max loaded the lawn mower into the pickup and drove on to his next lawn, Bilko in the seat beside him. Lawn mower, nice blue pickup, Bilko, is this all there is? Yes, and it was all he wanted. And when he was with Nelly and the kids in his yard, that's all he wanted, too. Then, as he took a left on to Thayer Road, he saw in the rearview mirror, or thought he saw, the soft eyes of the beautiful woman, and he wasn't so sure.

After lunch Max did Mrs. Parkland's place. A nice big lawn with towering oaks overhead. Max still had fantasies of having a tree house someday, and these oaks were perfect. A Swiss Family Robinson retirement place with all sorts of twisting wooden walkways and little rooms in among the branches.

Max liked Mrs. Parkland. She was a JFK buff like him, specializing in assassination theory. She had an entire wall in her den covered with Kennedy stuff—election posters, buttons, headlines, pictures from *Life* magazine. If Max ever tried anything like that, Nelly would have killed him. He was allowed one little porcelain JFK bust, which he kept on the TV because JFK was the first TV president.

Whenever Max did Mrs. Parkland's lawn, the spirit of

JFK hovered in the air and sometimes engaged Max in conversation.

"Afternoon, Max," came the familiar Boston accent from over behind the yews.

Max turned from his mower and looked into the shadows. A half-hidden figure in coat and tie lifted his hand in greeting.

"Mr. President! Good afternoon, sir."

"It's, uh, Jack to you, Max."

"Yes sir!"

"Boy, the inside of Mrs. Parkland's house is something. She's quite a fan."

"Well, we all were, Jack." Actually Max's age had only been in the single digits during JFK's term.

"Not all, I'm afraid. There was at least one person who wasn't a fan."

Did Oswald act alone? At last, the answer to the big question. He'd never have a chance like this again.

"Jack, there's something I have to ask."

JFK held up his hand. "Dallas, right? That's all right, it's the, uh, one they all ask. That, and was I really about to pull out of Vietnam." He pronounced Vietnam like ham.

"Well, you can forget Oswald. Oswald didn't act alone, or with anyone else. In fact, he had nothing to do with it."

Max's jaw dropped.

"That's right, nothing. Get ready for this one, Max. Where were we that day? In Texas. What kind of cops were in the motorcade? Texans. And who was the biggest Texan of them all, riding ten feet back in the car behind mine?"

"Johnson!" whispered Max.

"Hard to believe that man had the wit to do it. But he was eager—ol' Lyndon was one eager cowboy."

Johnson. He'd have to look at the Zapruder film again, it had to be there in that grainy footage. . . .

Then he heard a snort come from the yews, then a giggle, then a hysterical burst of laughter. It was a while before JFK could get himself under control.

"Oh, Max, Max, Max," he said, wiping the tears from his eyes, still laughing. "Johnson didn't do it. I'm just pulling your dick, son. Just pulling your dick. Forgive me, it was irresistible."

Max looked away, humiliated.

"Come on, now. It was, uh, just a joke. Max, you can't ask those questions until you come here yourself."

"Here?" said Max.

"Up here. The place where all good Catholics go. You are Catholic, aren't you, Max?" JFK snickered.

Max was almost afraid to ask, but he did anyway. "How is up there, Jack?"

"Pretty good, I suppose, pretty much how you'd expect. Of course, it's changed a little since Walt Disney came, but it's still nice." JFK began to fade. "Well, Max, I have to be on my way. We'll talk again soon. By the way," said the president, pointing with a nearly transparent finger, "you missed a little patch over there by the grassy knoll."

Three lawns later, Max finished up the day and headed home. Nelly was working first shift this week, so she had picked up Nora from day-care and was already there. He backed into the driveway and rolled the big Bearcat mower out of the pickup and pushed it into his workshop. The blade was off balance, the mower had been vibrating ever so slightly the last two lawns. Max had the blade off in a second, eyeballed it, then worked a file back and forth on either end. He didn't even check the balance before he put it back on because he knew he was right—he was an expert in his own little field, mower maintenance. While he was at it, he cleaned the air filter, regapped the spark plug, and tightened one of the bolts on the engine housing. The mower would last longer than he would, and that thought pleased and depressed him. No one would care as much as he had.

Nelly appeared, still in her whites, and they kissed, Nelly arching away so she wouldn't get grease on her.

"Promise me—when I die, you'll bury my mowers with me," said Max.

"Do you want me to shoot them first, or do you want them buried alive?" Nelly asked.

"Just remove their little spark plugs, that'll do the job."

Nelly looked fine in white. Whenever Max fantasized about her, she was always dressed in her uniform.

"How was your day?" he asked, meaning, What sort of patient muck did you get all over your white self today?

"The usual chaos," Nelly said cheerfully, "the usual concentration of unbelievable human misery."

"Good, huh?" he said.

"Actually, it started out bad, got worse, then one of my chronics coded and didn't make it—which was the good part." It made the nurses happy when a chronically ill patient finally died, and all the tubes could come out, the suffering stop. "This guy had one of those families who kept insisting we do everything possible. At the end he was just a respirator and a feeding tube."

Max put a hand up to block the flow of details. "Is there ever any good news in your job?"

"Sure there is," she said, taking his arm and leading him inside. "Today I fixed a guy's TV antenna."

Joan and Sam Widener came over after supper, and a few minutes after them, Billy Dalton showed up. Sam and Billy were old high school friends of Max's, and Billy, if a married man was allowed such an indulgence, was Max's best chum. But things were not as they once were between Max and Sam, or Sam and anyone for that matter, since he married Joan three years ago.

Sam was obsequious around his wife, and it disheartened Max and Billy to watch it. Joan overpowered him, or as Billy said, had him by the psychic nuts. If he even breathed funny, Joan was all over him.

The tension level of the evening had been reasonably low

until Sam said, "Think I'll have another one," and stood up, empty drink glass in hand.

"Honey . . . ," said Joan.

Max looked at Billy, Billy looked at Max. Nelly looked away. Joan's "honey" was the first step in an exquisitely choreographed dance of emotional death. It astounded Max that they so eagerly performed this dance in public. Such a performance belonged behind closed doors, Max felt, along with making babies and blowing your nose.

"What?" Sam replied good-naturedly, his mouth a little slack. Max could see in Sam's eyes, though, the frightened squint of a flinching animal about to be struck.

"Oh, nothing, go ahead," said Joan, smiling at him, then at everyone else in the living room.

Sam looked as if he was about to go ahead—his body at least signaled it—but Max knew there was more chance of a kodiak bear roaring through the front door than Sam making it into the kitchen to fix himself another drink. He actually made it halfway into the kitchen before turning to Joan.

"You don't think I should?" he said to her, wincing, because even he knew how bad he sounded. By this time Billy had gotten up and walked to a corner of the living room where he was showing great interest in a spider plant.

"No, no, do what you want," said Joan. Max's head was flicking back and forth between the players, like the crowd at Wimbledon.

Sam walked back into the living room, ice cubes tinkling feebly in his empty glass. "No, I guess you're right. I'm not really in the mood for another one." He dropped back down on the sofa, and the cushion beneath him let out an exasperated sigh.

Sam was not an alcoholic. The issue was not substance abuse. If Sam had expressed an interest in eating another cheese nacho or a second helping of guacamole dip, Joan would have proffered guidance and advice. What happens to your friends? Max wondered. Why do they, more often than not, select such awful partners?

When Sam and Joan left, Billy went into his Joan and Sam routine.

"I think I'll take a leak, dear," he said in his Sam voice.

"Do you think you should?" Billy said in a higher-register Joan imitation.

A pause. "Well, my bladder's pretty full. . . ."

"You know best. If your bladder's full, it's full."

"But it's not what I'd call *totally* full. It's more like it's a three-quarters-type thing."

"I can't urinate for you, Sam, you'll have to decide."

"No, you decide."

"Well, if you insist. Don't go to the bathroom."

Another pause, and a pained expression. "When, um, do you think I can go? When would it be convenient for you?"

"Sam, we'll talk about it again in the morning. Now don't bother me."

Nelly laughed, then said, "Do I ever Joan you, Max?"

"Never," he said. "We have the perfect marriage. Bladder autonomy is respected in this relationship."

Nelly went on up to bed and lay there thinking about Max's words. The perfect marriage. The words scared her a little. Perfect. Max saw perfection everywhere—in his gleaming mowers, the smiles of his children, the ears on his dog, his marriage. He was such a hopeful man. And she was too much the nurse, her outlook too guarded. She shifted to a cooler spot on the bed. It was not wise to ponder marriage after having watched three hours of the Sam and Joan show. She thought sleepily of Max and hoped he would come to bed soon.

Billy and Max had moved out to the front porch and sat rocking in the dark.

"You've got the last great wife in America, you know

that, don't you?" said Billy, opening a Rolling Rock. He took a swig, then burped.

"It seems that way, after tonight," said Max. "We're not really being fair, though. I admit Joan's a beast. But there are plenty of fine women out there."

"Name thirty fine women out there," said Billy, sucking down his Rolling Rock.

"Nancy DeLapp, Tarra Hopson, Betsy Pitts . . ." Max's voice faded.

"That's three, twenty-seven to go," said Billy. "I rest my case." He burped again.

Billy was between women, a perpetual state it seemed. He would latch on to some oddity and bring her around for inspection, then he'd spend the evening as tense as a cat, watching Max watch his date.

He would take Max aside and whisper things like: "You don't like her hair and she talks too much, right? Am I right?"

"Jesus, Billy, relax. Did I say anything?" In fact, Billy's date, Liane, *did* talk too much, and her hair, with actual pin curls around the ears, was alarming.

"What got in to me, Max? Why am I going out with her? Listen to her in there."

Liane was sitting on the sofa with Nelly, jabbering away. She was zooming through a variety of topics, Max barely following any of it. But Nelly was doing a good job with her, because she had shifted into her nurse mode. Nurse Nelly was treating Liane as a mildly disturbed patient, nodding and smiling through all the crazy talk.

"She seemed normal before I brought her here. But now . . . I can't go back out there, Max. I can't do it."

Somehow, they had gotten through that night, and others like it. Not all of Billy's women were so loony. Max and Nelly had liked a few of them and were always saddened when they disappeared from Billy's romantic agenda.

Annie was one of them. She laughed easily, smelled wonderfully of baby powder, and did not mind that Billy was a mailman or that he wore socks with his sandals. Billy had come slumping over one day, unable to look Max or Nelly in the face.

"Annie's gone," said Nelly, who was acute in such matters.

"Annie's gone," repeated Billy dully. "Do you have a sharp implement in your kitchen I could eviscerate myself with? Or some incredibly toxic household cleanser?"

"What happened?" said Max. Max, too, had had a quiet hankering for Annie. She was really likeable.

"Remember the guy from Cincinnati, the not-quite-resolved love affair? Well, it just got resolved. She's going back to him."

"No," said Max.

"Yes," said Billy. "He writes one shitty little letter, and *poof*, she's gone. I must mean a lot to her if all it takes is a twenty-two-cent stamp to buy her. Cincinnati, I can't even *spell* Cincinnati," Billy said, as if his inability to spell had somehow led to his downfall.

So there had been good ones, and bad ones, and every one of them Billy had shared with Max and Nelly.

"You know," Billy said, "if I ever try to marry a Joan, I want you to forcibly restrain me, get a court order. Whatever it takes."

"Impossible," said Max. "No one can stop a bad marriage."

"Yeah, I guess," said Billy, downing the last third of his frosty. "Why is that?" Then he said, "At least don't make fun of me like we make fun of Sam."

"I promise only to make fun of you behind your back, in the privacy of my own home, in the company of my legal wife."

"A wife like yours is so good she should be illegal," said Billy. "I want you to know," he said, "that if you die, are institutionalized, or are in any other manner incapacitated, I am going to marry your wife."

This was a subject they had been over before. Billy had professed his love for Nelly many times.

"Do you mean if I am wheelchair bound, you'll take my wife away from me?" said Max.

"No, that's handicapped. I said incapacitated. Unable to do anything but move your little finger and blink."

"You'll take my wife when I can still blink?" Max had a fleeting vision of Billy and Nelly saying their vows as he watched through a weak fluttering of his eyelids, as if the ceremony was being shown on a jittery 1930s newsreel.

"You bet. Life is cruel."

"What about Bilko?" said Max. "What about my lawn mowers?"

"Bilko will be sold to a vivisectionist to help defray the costs of the wedding. And your lawn mowers I'll give to Clement Strokas." Billy laughed gleefully.

"Not to Clement!" Clement Strokas ran one of the other lawn-mowing operations in Gramenton. His mowers spewed blackened smoke, engines sputtering from lack of maintenance. Max had once seen Clement kick a stubborn machine. It was a sight he would never forget.

Billy went inside to get another beer, and Max put his feet up on the front porch railing and watched as a car drove slowly past. As he watched, a familiar warm ocean smell reached his nose. He stood up. The car, a long purple convertible with fins, had no driver. Maybe it was a trick of the light as the car passed under a street lamp. And then the woman Max had seen in the rhododendrons sat up from the backseat as if half rising from bed. She raised a white arm and crooked a finger at Max, beckoning.

Billy came back out as the car disappeared into the night.

Max stood looking out onto the street.

"What's the matter with you?" said Billy, when Max neither moved nor spoke.

"Would you marry Nelly," said Max, in a voice that was hardly his own, "if I cheated on her?"

Billy snorted. "If you cheated on her, I'd shoot you first, then I'd marry her. But you wouldn't, so there's nothing to worry about. Right?"

"What?" said Max. He could barely follow the conversation. What was he talking about?

Billy eyed him. "You sound like you either need a beer or you've had one too many." He was quiet a minute, then said, "You aren't about to do something stupid, are you? Something I'd have to shoot you for?"

Max laughed, his head clearing. "I just saw a beautiful woman drive by in a car." He did not give details or say that he had also seen her in the rhododendrons.

Billy was relieved. "Beautiful women in cars are okay," he said. "Because they drive by and keep going. Specific beautiful women with names and addresses are not okay."

"Hey, don't you trust me?" said Max.

"Hey, you sounded weirder than usual for a second," said Billy.

They talked on into the summer night as old friends do and drank beers until the conversation slurred into silence. Then Billy mounted his old red three-speed bike and pedaled his zigzag way home.

3

*M*AX decided, after all, to go on vacation.

"Let's go to Peleg's Island," he'd said to Nelly a few nights after his midnight drunk with Billy. "Let's go to the beach."

"I thought you wanted to stay home all summer," Nelly said. Vacation, however, suited her. She was getting sick of the hospital. There had been an exceptionally high influx of gorks lately.

"I don't know, for some reason I'm ready for Peleg's. Besides, it hasn't really rained in weeks and the grass is slow. Now's a good time to go."

Max's grandmother owned an old beach house on Peleg's, off the South Carolina coast. Max had been going down since he was a few months old, and almost every year for the past thirty-two years. Peleg's lived in Max's subconscious the way important places do, so that it was no longer simply Peleg's but was the memory of Peleg's, too, of long ago vacations and childhood—the past and present were simultaneous.

There were always three parts to those childhood vacations: the long drive down (Max never remembered the drive back home), the side trip to see Grandma Lakeman, and the weeks on Peleg's Island.

Oh, that annual ritual, the sweltering six-hundred-mile drive down U.S. 1—down I-95 once it was built—to South

Carolina. Emmett at the wheel squinting into the sun, Phillies cap on his brow even though the interior of the car was hot enough to bake biscuits. Doris in the passenger's seat, placating an overheated husband and entertaining two restless and excited little boys. And Max in the backseat with his brother, Fred.

Max and Fred were extremely territorial. On long trips the seat was divided down the exact middle, Max on the right, Fred on the left. There were incredible border disputes, with the two brothers whacking each other and yelling to protest illegal crossings. Emmett carried a cherry stick tucked under his window visor which he often used, flailing blindly behind him as he drove, to quell backseat riots. He never hit Max and Fred, but the threat was enough to subdue them for five or ten miles.

There were a number of unspoken car rules, all Emmett's and all unreasonable. Two of the most excruciating were: 1) no stopping, and 2) no eating in transit. Talk about torture. Emmett's idea of a car ride was you got in at point A and you didn't get back out until you reached point B. Between the two points nothing existed, not restaurants, not points of historical interest, and especially not rest areas. Woe unto the child in need before arrival at point B. The conversations were always the same:

FRED: "Max has to pee."

MAX: "I do not!" (In truth, Fred had to, but he was not fool enough to admit it.)

EMMETT: Silence. A sigh. Silence.

DORIS: "Max, are you sure?"

MAX: "I don't have to, Fred does!"

FRED: "He told me he did, and I do too, now." (A beautiful move. Double your little brother's criminality.)

Everybody looks at Emmett.

DORIS (finally, in almost a whisper): "I think the boys have to go, dear."

EMMETT: "Give 'em a Dixie cup."

DORIS: "I will not give them Dixie cups."

EMMETT: "Christ, didn't they go before we left?"

DORIS: "That was two hundred and fifty miles ago! It will take you exactly one minute to pull this car over and let your sons go to the bathroom."

EMMETT: "If they were my sons, they wouldn't have to go to the bathroom."

DORIS: "You're impossible!"

Emmet drums his fingers on the steering wheel and broods for about five miles. The pressure in Max's bladder, for no reason other than Fred's power of suggestion, increases. He is about to seriously panic when his father suddenly pulls over onto the gravel shoulder of the road sending them all bouncing around in the car. He turns his red sweaty face to the backseat and growls, "You have exactly thirty seconds, and don't give me any guff."

The other rule, not eating, was where Doris revealed, yet again, her saintliness. Emmett, being fussy and neat, did not allow snacking in the car. Would it have killed him to let Max and Fred have a little something? Well, rules were rules, and Doris, to the eternal gratitude of her boys, broke the rules. She started every long trip with her pocketbook weighted down with LifeSavers, M&M's, Cracker Jacks, and Tootsie Rolls. And as the miles rolled inexorably by, she'd slide the candy down under the front seat to the hungry captives in the back.

Doris had one little rule of her own: if Daddy caught you, you were on your own. As a result, Max had learned the fine survival techniques of the muffled chew and the silent candy wrapper removal. He sometimes thought of himself as a silent Indian walking through dangerous forests, where the snap of a dry twig or the crackle of a Tootsie Roll wrapper could cost him his life.

Down, down, down that long, lonesome road into Dixie. The whole family, in fact, with Emmett taking the strong lead, actually whistled "Dixie" when they crossed the border from North to South Carolina. It was a song of expectation and relief—the hellish ride would soon come to an end, and phase two, visiting Grandma Lakeman, was about to begin.

After he crossed the South Carolina border Emmett would turn off the highway and drive the back roads that led to Grandma. This, for Max, was when the reality of the South hit. Max would get very quiet those last few miles, the sense of otherworldliness commanding his attention. The air smelled of road heat and pine; the soil was red sand; the land lay flat and shimmering in the undiluted sun. The tiny towns they'd pass through all looked the same, drab two-story brick storefronts hunched along the main street. At stoplights Max would hear snatches of conversation as the townspeople, moving listlessly in the bright heat, went about their unknown business. The way they talked, who could understand them! Fred imitated their accents, and they laughed at the strangeness until Emmett shushed them. Their chatter interrupted his own sensations, his own drift back into a world that had long ago somehow been his home.

So close to Grandma's now. There would be a few more towns, and a few more tobacco fields, each with one decaying tobacco barn amid the dusty green rows. The barns were so old, rusty tin roofs, brown weathered pine—everything here seemed old to Max, the buildings, the fields, the people making their slow way down broken sidewalks in front of the Winn Dixie supermarkets, the Baptist churches, the Esso filling stations with their two tired blue pumps.

And then Grandma's, where the world was familiar and alive again. The trees lining her street were huge, their thick limbs covered with gray lichen. The long drive was almost over, and Fred and Max went ape, freely crossing backseat borders that had been unbreachable for six hundred miles, hanging out the window, laughing and punching each other's arms. Then Grandma's house, white brick, sprawling beneath the shade of pecan and pine trees. They were there.

Max and Fred would charge out of the car trying to be

the first to reach Grandma's door. It was always the back door they went to—the front, with its wide brick steps, was used only for formal occasions. Grandma was there at the door, always, and she'd open it and step back to avoid the heat. Max would go up on his toes to kiss her, and she'd stoop to him and turn her head slightly away, in the manner of women who kiss frequently in greeting. He'd smell her hair then, her pale pink skin, her clean flowered dress. She'd kiss the rest of them, and Max would steal away to walk through the cool dark house, to have a few minutes by himself to make sure everything was still there, to make sure everything was exactly as it had been the year before. And it always was. The shades were drawn in all the rooms to keep the cool in, so that wandering around in the dimness among the dark ornate furniture, Max felt as if he was in a rarely visited corner of a museum where the exhibits never changed.

Although Grandma's house might have been creepy, it rarely was, except for moments alone in the bedtime dark with his glasses off and his spook vision going full tilt. There was certainly nothing scary about Grandma. She was old of course, and old usually means scary to a child, and formal, and that can be kind of scary, too. But she'd do silly things for Fred and Max, make faces and funny noises, take out her partial dentures at bedtime and let her long white hair out of its tight bun and pretend to be the wicked witch.

Of all the traditions, the Bavarian cream pie, the supreme Grandma dessert, was the most eagerly anticipated. Max and Fred talked about it all year long, worked themselves up to such a level of expectation that it was practically impossible for them to sit through the annual Lakeman family meal.

"You boys just settle down," Doris would say to her fidgeting sons.

Settle down? Max imagined in Grandma's refrigerator a Bavarian cream pie four feet across, the custard golden yellow, the ladyfingers sparkling with sugar. He was supposed to settle down?

Finally, the grown-ups finished their meals and Grandma stood up. Emmett, as he did every year, would say, "How about we go over to the Dairy Freeze and I'll get you guys some chocolate cones?"

"Nooo, nooo!" Max would holler.

"You don't want dessert?" He'd turn to Grandma. "Mother, these boys don't want dessert."

"We do. We do!" It was excruciating, this delay.

"Oh, Emmett, you stop now," Grandma would say, setting out her pink Depression glass plates, then walking slowly into the dining room with the Bavarian cream pie held out in front of her. At the sight of it Max would catch his breath and turn to Fred, who was for once too overcome to speak.

Precisely two days later they'd get back in the car for the short trip to Peleg's Island on the South Carolina coast. It always seemed to be low tide when they got to Peleg's, and the smell of marsh mud and sea air would make them giddy as it poured into the car. The island was three miles long, a quarter mile wide, and had a tidal creek on one side emptying into the ocean at either end. The beach house was on the creek side.

Max was always the first one out of the car. He had to see the place, inspect it the way he inspected Grandma's. It was change he was looking for, and unlike Grandma's, change was evident everywhere here. The old house, which Max touched in greeting, would be missing shingles; sand was blown in onto the back screened porch; the dock was older and even more rickety; its lopsided pilings had continued their slow accumulation of oysters and barnacles. Out front on the beach, the dunes he and Fred had played among last year were going, or gone, and new dunes to be explored had risen from the sand.

The days passed slowly on Peleg's. Doris read magazines, watched the egrets walking in the marsh grass, and reluctantly cleaned and cooked the fish and clams and shrimp Emmett and the boys brought in from the creek. Emmett was a man on the move. He swam two or three times a day, repaired the crab nets, fished. Vacationed with a vengeance. Perhaps it was because he was a conductor, confined to the same train day after day, and now that he was off the train, he had no intention of wasting his freedom.

Peleg's was the first place in Max's life that suggested the relentless strangeness of the world. The creatures of the creek and sea, for one thing, were very strange. All those feelers, and claws, and bizarre shapes and sizes, the skins that were hard or slimy, the protruding eyeballs, the phosphorescent glow of the night sea. The lesson was clear. Be wary. Don't think you've seen it all, because out there, out there in the creek and in the vast hissing ocean, lurked the truly unknown.

The ocean itself taught the strangeness lesson. Max would stare and stare, not knowing what to make of all that moving water. He didn't fool around with it, that's for sure. No amount of coaxing from Emmett or taunts from Fred would induce him to go in above his waist. Waist high the warm green waves were luscious, but deeper than that the water was not his friend.

At night Max would lay on the army cot on the back porch peering at the dark creek. He felt like the only living being in the world. Sometimes, lying out there, he would see a point of light jiggling way down along the banks of the creek. This would always scare the living bejesus out of him. The light would glide closer, and then he'd begin to hear hushed voices and low laughter, and the soft sound of oars pulling through the water. The Death Boat coming to get him. That is what it looked and sounded like to a myopic boy alone on the darkened porch. But it was only the black fishermen gigging for flounder, their lanterns shining into the shallow water along the bank. The Death Boat, this time, had passed him by. Oh, the strangeness of the world.

So once again to Peleg's Island, with Max now in the Emmett role of father, and Nelly and Nora and Ben. And

Bilko. The trip began, as always, with packing the night before. Max attacked the job prissily, neatly, as he did most things. Nelly, who understood that in the grand scheme, precision packing was not that high up there, jammed children's supplies and toys into pillowcases, and her own things into a bedraggled backpack.

Max stood back as Nelly threw her stuff into the back of the Chevette. They did not speak. He waited until she went back inside for the next load, then took out what she had tossed in and began to methodically repack. Okay, toys up close to the front in case the kids needed them, clothes in back, Bilko's food in back, map up front, fishing pole on the side, no hooks sticking out, right? Right. Leave space for the cooler to go in in the morning, clear a spot for Bilko. Remember to bring water and leash.

Nelly was standing behind him, another load in her arms.

"Everything at right angles?" she said, dropping her load at the curbside. "That box over there doesn't look parallel to the one next to it."

"I know you find my packing amusing," said Max.

"No," said Nelly. "Sexy. I find a man who packs a car like you do very, very sexy."

"Yeah?"

"Yeah. God, I could watch you for hours. The way you rearrange those suitcases. Gives me goose bumps."

"Well," said Max, going along, "I guess it's a talent pretty much like anything else."

"Talent? We're talking genius." She wrapped her arms around him and breathed, "And genius is very sexy."

"You're just trying to distract me," Max said squirming.

"From what?" Nelly murmured.

"From the fact that you pack like a three-year-old."

"Hah!" said Nelly, pulling away and stomping back to the house. "Hah. See if you get any M&Ms from me tomorrow. See if you get any Cracker Jacks or Tootsie Rolls." She knew Max's stories down to the tiniest detail, because of course, for Max the tiniest detail was the most important one.

The agony of trying to sleep the night before. Max tossed, listening to clocks tick, children sigh, dogs snore, and Nelly, blissfully asleep while he drummed his fingers on the headboard. Midnight, oh, God, twelve-thirty—why, when he needed rest so badly, was there no rest to be had? One A.M., and then, *ping*, his eyes closed, *ping* again, it was 5:00 A.M., and his digital watch alarm was chirping beside his ear.

Nelly popped out of bed, refreshed, ready for action, while he lay there trying to force open eyes that were stapled shut with fatigue.

"Morning, honey bunch sugar lump," said Nelly blithely, as Max eased himself into the kitchen.

"Daddy, we're going to Peleg's Island!" shouted Ben, whapping his spoon down into his bowl of Cheerios. Cheerios was a name Max presently found offensive.

"Daddy!" said Nora, unable to complete a sentence, but still getting points for enthusiasm.

Only Bilko treated him tenderly. Bilko said nothing, merely licked the side of his leg as he passed by.

"You know the rules, Nelly," he said, his eyes puffy slits. "No one talks to me before Baltimore." By Baltimore he would be awake, jarred into attention by the trucks bearing down on him from behind.

Five-thirty A.M. and they were in the car, ready to go. Max went over the checklist with Nelly, pilot to copilot. Nelly nodded affirmatively each time.

"Change for tolls?" said Max.

"Check."

"Water for Bilko? Leash?"

"Check."

"Ice chest? Sunglasses? Tylenol?"

"Check, check, check."

"Map?"

"Map?" said Nelly. "What do you need a map for? You've driven the same way for thirty years."

"Thirty-two. Map?" he said looking at her.

"No map," said Nelly. "Abort takeoff, I repeat, abort takeoff."

"Map," said Max, reaching over her lap into the glove compartment. "You think I'd trust you?" He produced a map.

"You're a dink," she said.

"You'll thank me when we hit a detour that takes us out to Nowheresville, North Carolina," said Max. "Doors locked, seatbelts fastened? This old bird is ready to fly."

And so they flew, as much as a loaded-down vacation-bound Chevette can fly, down the interstate. The sun rose through pink clouds as they neared the Baltimore Harbor Tunnel. Max was awake, Nelly was staring out the window in her trip trance, the children were conked out in the back. Traffic was just beginning to pick up, but for the time being they were safe.

"Suckers!" Max said to those who, unlike him, would soon be caught in rush-hour tunnel traffic. He liked the tunnel, with its mesmerizing tiled walls. It was like going back in time, like he would end up in a cornfield in the 1800s when he came out at the other end.

Bilko climbed over the front seat and wedged herself in between Max and Nelly. Max scrunched over so she'd have more room. It was a bit warm to have a hairy body next to him, but Max was accommodating, especially since he understood long car rides puzzled Bilko. He knew that as attentive as Bilko was to the passing scenery, climbing in the car in Gramenton and out again on Peleg's Island rattled her. How'd we get here? her worried face said as she sniffed salt air and sand dunes. It confused Max a little, too. You sit still in the car for twelve hours, things go by, houses and trees and so on, and then you get out of the car, and you are somewhere else. And sometime else, too. It was the kind of problem you probably got in physics, which is why he never took physics.

The Washington Beltway was not as pleasant, and the comfortable feeling he'd had back at the tunnel disappeared. The sun was up now, the heat would begin soon.

"You want me to drive?" said Nelly

"No, I'm all right for now." Goddamned trucks, he thought. That game of chicken they play coming right up your ass as if they'll run you over if you don't move. All those truckers were half-crazed on speed—Christ knew what the road looked like to them after driving eighteen straight hours. Probably hallucinating, every one of them, not able to tell his Chevette from a bump in the road. Max pulled over and three semis screamed past him.

"Daddy, let's sing a song," said Ben.

"Daddy's busy right now," said Max, admiring his son's ability to pick the wrong moment.

Nelly led Ben in something from some children's daytime TV show Max had never heard. Max quietly hummed a song from a show he had once watched: "Mighty Mouse." He wished Mighty Mouse would come to his rescue, save him from the trucks.

At last, off the beltway, and on, in more amiable traffic, to Richmond.

"Rest area," said Ben, recognizing the blue signs. Max, flying in the face of the Emmett tradition, stopped at all the rest areas.

"Okay, José," said Max. He pulled into the hot parking lot and opened the door. Bilko bounded out over him, and Max peeled himself from the sweaty seat, got out of the car, and stretched. Nelly went off to drain the children.

A few parking spaces down he heard the sound of a man and woman arguing. They spoke exotic words he did not understand. The man, in all this heat, was dressed in a white tuxedo. His hair was thick gray and curly, his eyebrows fierce.

The woman's back was turned, Max couldn't see her face. It wasn't until they'd slammed their doors and driven off that Max realized he had seen that purple convertible with the big fins before. He sniffed nervously, but nothing came to him except the hot Virgina air.

Nelly came back from the restrooms holding Nora and Ben by the hands.

"Where's Bilko?" she said.

"What?" said Max, still staring into the distance.

"Ground control to Max."

"Daddy's lost Bilko," said Ben.

"Bilko," said Nora, her face scrunching up.

Max turned and perused the questioning faces of his family.

At that moment Bilko came tearing over to them from a cluster of picnic tables. She was carrying something in her mouth. Behind her, running with considerably less grace, came an irate, red-faced man.

Uh-oh, thought Max, instant sweat to his armpits, confrontation time. Bilko ran right up to him and sat, so there was no use pretending he wasn't her owner, which of course had been his first impulse. Bilko held a Baggie with a sandwich in it between her teeth.

The man, coming to a halt in front of him, shouted, "Is that your goddamned dog?" Nelly, with Ben and Nora, stepped gingerly behind Max, the family protector. Max gave her a look.

Hoping his voice didn't sound squeaky, Max said, "Yes, I'm afraid this is my dog."

"Yeah, well, see that sign, it says, Dogs Must Be Leashed." The man's face was thick and ugly, a face built for just this type of situation.

"She got away." It was the best Max could do.

"She got away," the face growled back.

Nelly whispered behind Max, "Tell him to go fuck himself."

Max managed a weak smile as he waited for the blows to start raining down on him. But the man, miraculously, had not heard. Praise be to God, Max spotted a little pink hearing aid in his right ear.

Max yanked the Baggie from Bilko's reluctant jaws. It was covered with dog spit.

"I'm sorry," said Max.

"Sorry's not good enough."

"Sorry's all I've got," Max said.

It was a moment of high drama. The man was obviously inclined toward violence. Max looked around for a weapon. The nearest thing was a gray metal trash can. He had visions of being jammed, headfirst, into the trash can.

Then Ben, bless his little soul, pointed to the red-faced man and said, "Look, Daddy. He has a hat just like Grandpa's."

The man touched his straw hat and made a kind of grunting sound.

"Do you know my grandpa?" Ben said to the man.

The man looked at Ben quickly, then back to Max. "Okay. Just next time you watch your goddamned dog." Then he stomped off back to his picnic table.

"You bet," Max called after him.

"I would first of all like to thank my dog, Bilko," said Max, when they were on the road again, "for her wonderful public behavior." Bilko, hearing her name mentioned, barked happily from the backseat.

"And for Best Supporting Role in a Crisis, I would like to nominate my lovely and unhelpful helpmate, Nelly Lakeman. . . . Next time we come face to face with a psychopath," he went on, "please do not issue instructions for him to go fuck himself."

"It was irresistible," said Nelly.

"He wanted to damage your husband."

"It would never have happened," said Nelly confidently, squeezing his leg.

"Oh, and why not?"

"Because my husband would have run far, far away."

Max had no argument with that one. "Now I know why my father never stopped at rest areas," he said.

Through Richmond and its endless twenty-five-cent tollbooths, Max handed out petty cash to a succession of dazed tollbooth guards. He smiled and nodded to these people and looked approvingly at them, trying to bring a bit of cheer to their dull lives. He never got a response, not a twitch of life, only the robot hands reaching for the change.

"It's because they're brain dead," said Nelly. "It's a job requirement."

"I think the exhaust impairs them," Max said more charitably. "Could you imagine inhaling that stuff all day?"

"Worse, could you imagine handling that money all day?"

"Jesus, you're right." Max, having had it instilled into him long ago by Doris, was convinced if you put your finger in your mouth after touching a coin, you would contract a hideously terminal disease that manifested itself in open sores on your face.

They drove peacefully for a time, Nora and Ben not being old enough yet to create the backseat commotions that in coming years would surely dominate all long car trips. Max amused himself with billboards. His favorites were the ones advertising caves and caverns. They were always gaudy and worn, with their fading pictures of huge stony vaults and dazzling stalactites. Rainbow Cave. What a name, still drew him in, sucker romantic that he was. He imagined hundred-foot ceilings, bottomless pools that glowed a mineral blue, multicolored stalactites stretching endlessly into the dark, the echoes, that cool hidden smell. The only cave he had ever been to was years ago on a field trip with the Boy Scouts. Big Bear Cave. Big Bear Cave had not amounted to much: a large room with a sort of stale urine smell and a spotlight shining down on a stalagmite, a lumpy pile Max supposed was the bear. The bear what? Hibernating, squatting, dead? In fact, he'd been to

Carlsbad Caverns, too, and that was spectacular, but the only thing he remembered was limping along endlessly in the dark, hobbled by his flourishing case of athlete's foot.

"Rain," said Nelly.

Huge drops, fat as bugs, splattered on the windshield. Max had been thinking about the purple convertible, about caves, and he had not seen the quick change from blue sky to gray.

He immediately slowed down. The most dangerous time to drive, when the road was wet and greasy, before it rained hard enough to wash away the oil. Steam rose from the asphalt, the wheels on the car ahead of Max's were lost in it.

"I love it," said Nelly.

"Yeah, me, too," said Max, licking his lips, so intent on safety, looking so hard down the road it was as if he was trying to see into the future. Which in a way, he was—accidents of the future.

Nelly had the window down and her arm stretched way out. "The way it hits your hand, it stings but doesn't hurt."

Max sniffed. The road *did* smell good. Somehow organic, and satisfying. But dangerous, no time to let down your guard. He put on his emergency flashers.

"We're underwater, Daddy," chirped Ben from the backseat. "We're in a marine."

"*Sub*marine," said Nelly.

A hot line of lightning flashed over a tobacco field. Bilko leapt into the front seat and tried to hide behind Max's legs. There was a tense moment or two as Nelly struggled with the dog in the swerving car.

"Right out of *Accident* magazine," snapped Max when things were back under control. *Accident* magazine was something along the lines of the Church of the Scary Jesus Christ, another, though slightly different, creation of Max's mind evoked by the precarious events that riddled everyday life. Whenever he or Nelly or Emmett or Billy or anyone did something obviously stupid, like unplug a lamp with wet hands or reach beyond the safety zone of an extended ladder, Max would say, "There's one for *Accident* magazine. Yep, that's a real cover story, that move." Dog jumping under the driver's legs came under the section of the magazine entitled, "You Never Thought It Could Happen to You." Wet hands and ladders came under "Stupidity and You: Striving for a Premature Death."

Miles later, practically right on the North Carolina–South Carolina border, the rain ended. "It's a sign," said Max. "The gods are kindly disposed toward this journey." He broke into a lively rendition of "Dixie," in the Lakeman tradition. Nelly loyally tried to join him, but she whistled, as always, as if she had just eaten a box of saltines. Ben tried, too, but after the first few bars, his tune soon veered off into something complicated and atonal.

Ben whistled on in a solo for a minute and then, nose pressed against his backseat window, cried, "South of the Border! Can we go?"

Ah, that familiar plea, Max recognized in it his own youth. South of the Border, that gaudy eternal Mexican carnival, that temple of unadulterated commercialism. It stood, as its name truthfully stated, in fact the only truth of the whole place, just inside the South Carolina border. It was a place only a child could love, unless of course the child was of Mexican origin. There were rides, fireworks stores, fast-food outlets, miniature golf, water slides, endless crapola, all in a Mexican theme, and everywhere lazy Mexican statues leading lazy donkey statues to pointless destinations. It was beyond offensive, it was a work of degenerate art. How he had yearned to go when he was small. He could not see the dark side, only the magic, the living dream. But his father was Emmett Lakeman, and there was no stopping.

And there would be no stopping now. Max was an indulgent father, a softy, an easy touch, but South of the Border scared him because it was alluring and perverse, like Playland in Pinocchio. Those plaster donkey statues, for all he knew, *were* Pinocchio and his school chums, or some other group of hapless child captives. Ben would not be hee-hawing among them.

Nelly took the heat for him. "Ben, we can't stop. Grandma Lakeman's waiting for us."

"Awww," said Ben, his voice a defeated whine, "we never get to." Little Ben, have you been on this planet long enough to know about never?

The last leg to Grandma's, the back roads, the terminal small southern towns, dying, dying, but never quite dead, like the gorks in Nelly's hospital. The inhabitants still at the stoplights, still talking in their strange lilting way. Max looked in the rearview mirror and saw Ben wide-eyed and listening, trying to comprehend as Max had once tried to comprehend. He saw Ben's lips move and knew that he was trying to master the new language that drifted in the window to him.

The oaks still stood on Grandma Lakeman's street, though their leaves seemed thinner now, the Spanish moss more gray. And there was the white brick house, huge and sturdy and, from a distance at least, unmarred by the passage of time.

Ben jumped out of the car, followed by Nora and Bilko, and ran up the back steps. A heavy black woman came to the door, Mrs. Winston, Grandma's helper.

"Miss Lakeman just waking up," she said. "She got to have some time."

Max wasn't sure exactly what that meant, except that Grandma Lakeman was now very old. Ninety-one. It wasn't the same coming here anymore, the museum world of Grandma had finally, as hard as Max wished to staunch the flow of time, changed.

Mrs. Winston saw Max looking around. "It's just me, Mr. Lakeman, and I do the best I can."

"Of course," said Max, embarrassed, "I didn't mean . . ." But she was gone, off to attend to Grandma. He poked around the rooms. The furniture had smears of hastily wiped dust;

there was a stain on the sofa; a curtain was coming undone at the hem. Max swallowed.

Nelly came up behind him and put her arms around him. Even the children were quiet.

"Miss Lakeman will see you now," came the voice from a doorway.

Grandma sat up in bed, lost among the sheets and pillows.

"Fred, you come to see me?" she said in a voice so thin and breathless Max could barely make out the words.

"No, I'm Max," he said, kissing her pale cheek. It was cool. He turned to Mrs. Winston with a questioning look.

"She been doing that," said Mrs. Winston.

"Max?" said Grandma, as if she had never heard the name before. "Max, lax, stacks, packs," she said, adding his name to a jumble of words that meant nothing to her.

Nelly squeezed his hand.

"Racks, ax, cracks," Grandma went on, her voice failing.

"Cracker Jacks!" said Ben brightly, trying to enter the game.

"That you, Fred?" said Grandma, hearing Ben's voice.

"Fred's not here," Max said. "I'm . . ." But he did not try again.

"Fred, Freddy. Come close, come close so I can see you."

Max bent down beside her. "Don't ever," she said, her voice suddenly strong, "don't ever get old, Freddy. It's the shits." Then her eyes closed, and she was asleep.

"She been saying them dirty words," said Mrs. Winston, as they got ready to leave. "She been talking plenty."

They didn't stay the night at Grandma Lakeman's. In the car on the last miles to Peleg's Island, Nelly said, "People get old, Max."

After a moment he said, "Yeah, it's the shits."

They looked at each other and smiled.

It was twilight when they crossed the bridge from the mainland to Peleg's. The smell of the marsh drifted into the open windows, and fatigued and buzzed from the miles as he was, Max's spirits soared. Peleg's at least was a constant, was a dependable source of joy. Max slept well that first night, lulled by the sounds of the creek and the distant crash of waves on the beach, eased by the comforting presence of Nelly twitching slightly in her sleep, as she journeyed through a dreamscape of her own.

Days on the beach, days on the pier, days on the back porch watching the creek flow. In the morning Max would pull on a pair of cutoffs and he was dressed for the day. Nelly wore shorts and a tank top, a combination that, for a man with simple erotic tastes, was endlessly appealing. Something about Nelly's costume, the salt air, the sea smells, whetted Max's appetite for physical contact.

"Again?" said Nelly in mock horror, one afternoon when the children were napping. "You're insatiable."

"I admit it," Max whispered, easing a strap down over her shoulder, "I am an animal." He nuzzled her nipple with his nose.

"Where'd you learn that?" said Nelly, her eyes closing. "From Bilko?"

The old bed rattled and creaked with their sweaty efforts.

"Jeepers," said Max, staring at her. "You're wonderful."

"Am I?" said Nelly. "Dull me, mother of two, big hips and all? Say it again."

"O big-hipped mother of two, you are wonderful." He kissed her sweetly, and then the old beach house filled once again with the sound of sighs and creaking springs.

Days with his children. Nora eating sand, marsh grass, a piece of bread she found blowing along the beach. Holding on to her in the water, looking down on her curly head as Emmett must have once looked down on his. It scared Max sometimes, that she trusted him so completely. She knew, assumed as only children assume, that he would never let her go to drift away in the water, that in his daddy arms she was safe forever.

For Ben, Peleg's was a big treasure chest, and he would bring Max and Nelly handfuls of ocean debris. The ocean didn't give Ben the willies as it did Max. He was fearless in the water, would swim out to the horizon and beyond if Max didn't grab him by the trunks and pull him back to safety. Did fear skip a generation? Emmett would sometimes swim at night, Max watching with pounding heart from the shore as his father's dark figure splashed in the phosphorescent glow of the night water. Ben, Max knew, would someday swim at night, too, while Max was forever locked on land.

For Bilko, Peleg's was a vast trash can, full of entrancing nasties to be eaten or rolled in. Fish carcasses, old shrimp bait tossed on the beach by the black fisherman on the end of the island, dead sand crabs. Eat it or wear it? Bilko faced such decisions countless times during her day. Sometimes, unobserved, Max saw her on her back, legs kicking in the air, twisting and writhing in ecstasy as she worked yet another revolting substance into her fur. Max felt like a worker at a toxic waste dump, handling Bilko at arm's length, pushing her into the shower once or twice a day.

"You are a man of infinite patience," said Nelly, watching him shower his dog.

"So true, so true," sighed Max.

"I'd be tempted to shoot her," Nelly said, wrinkling her nose at the aroma.

Wet and dripping Bilko eyed her with disdain.

"Nope, she's doing what she's got to do," he said. "She's just putting on a little doggie perfume. Doing what any single girl at the beach would."

"I'm curious to see what kind of date she ends up with."

"As a matter of fact," said Max stepping back as Bilko shook herself, "I happen to know a certain Jack Russell terrier that has a fondness for her."

"Don't you think she's a bit old for dating? Isn't she

lacking—how should I put it delicately—certain reproductive equipment?"

Max covered Bilko's ears. "Don't! I've never told her."

Nelly sat alone on the pier, her feet propped on the railing. Behind her, in the house, the children squealed as Max chased them through the rooms. She knew that he would be wearing some improvised costume, something involving wet towels and dirty sheets, probably her sunglasses, too, which no doubt were about to be lost or broken. An osprey circled far off to the right, then dropped down, lost in the tall green marsh grass. Nelly watched it, then stared at the marsh. She thought of Max examining the expanse of green with a professional eye.

Thoughts of Max. Peleg's overwhelmed him. It was the same every year. The trip down, Grandma Lakeman's, the house and island—there was too much for him to take in. There were so many emotional details, his brain, she knew, quivered with overload. When she married Max, she married a human nerve ending. She could usually follow him, keep up with his mental excursions, but there was always a point where he left her behind.

Really, she thought, Max was a small, safe man. Her life with him was remarkably dull. Barbecues, playing with the children, reading at night on the sofa. For Max, life *had* to be dull, because of the way he transformed ordinary events in his mind. Like walking Bilko. She had listened, over the years, to countless complicated conversations he had had with Bilko. Nelly wondered what she had given up by choosing to live with a man who wrapped himself so tightly in the lesser things.

The osprey rose again from the marsh. Lesser things that only seemed lesser. Now, with the sun on her, the osprey winging toward the ocean, her children noisy and happy in the house—her mood was lifted by the ordinary, and she knew why she had married Max. Her nervous thoughts left her for the moment, and she stood, stretched, and made her way up the back steps to join her family.

Max had a habit of viewing present events within the context of the future. So he was already looking back on this trip to Peleg's Island, not yet even over, as if it had occurred in some distant past. He was excruciatingly happy. He and Nelly were young and healthy, his two children were even younger and, presumably, healthier. Bilko, though no longer young, was at least highly energetic, and in every way a delightful friend and companion. Max imagined a benign god resting his golden arm around his shoulders, guiding him through an endlessly charmed life. Boy, remember how great it all was, Max was saying to himself, remember that time on Peleg's when it was Good? Boy, remember, remember?

Max wandered by himself up and down the beach in the twilight. In formation above the water six pelicans with fat bellies flew past, an arrow pointing toward the setting sun. Farther out, a school of dolphins arched into the air in unison, then disappeared into the water. Max found a dune and rested his back against the warm sand. He uncovered a small, bright shell with his toe. He remembered it all over again, his wife, his children, this moment; he remembered the moment, the exquisiteness of it, even as it was happening. As he gazed out at the ocean, he was full and empty at the same time.

Beyond the gentle green waves, something began to emerge from the water. Max, slowly coming to, stared. The water, in a circle perhaps five feet wide, began to glow as if lit below by blue and red lights. He thought he heard a kind of music, too, but perhaps it was only the wind moving through the dune grass. He looked around the beach but saw no one else. Then he looked again at the water, although he did not want to. *Run, run.* But he didn't run, he stared. Now a woman's head came into view, lifted out of the waves, her open eyes meeting his own. She continued to rise, slowly, the water streaming from her skin. Behind her the dolphins circled and splashed in play, and above her the pelicans reappeared and showered her with pink and white flowers they carried in their swollen bills. Petals fell on her auburn hair, they came to rest on her slight shoulders, on her breasts, on her magnificent hips. And still she rose, a radiant sun, until at last she was fully revealed, standing lightly in the center of a giant half shell, the blue shell of a scallop. A warm, scented breeze blew back her hair, her eyebrows lifted and her lips parted as if she were about to ask Max a question.

It was a question Max never heard. He stood up, did a sort of pirouette as his legs gave out from under him, and collapsed against the soft sand of the dune. When he opened his eyes, he thought the woman from the sea was covering his face with wet kisses. But his eyes focused instead on the pink and black nose of Bilko as she licked his cheek, then stepped back and eyed him nervously.

4

DON'T de days get by. Now it was the end of July, the hellish sauna of midsummer had wrapped its sweaty arms around Gramenton. The maple trees were spitting wet droplets of something, but Billy could not figure out what. Sap, tree perspiration? Billy didn't like to be spat on, he knew from personal experience. Once, he'd been spat on as he walked past a gang of young toughs hanging outside the 7-Eleven. He was fourteen or so, and the attack, such as it was, had been unprovoked, at least that's how Billy saw it. But to his attackers, Billy must have been asking for it: he was younger, he had zits, and he was wearing white athletic socks with sandals.

"Hey, queer bait," one of them had said to Billy.

Billy made a big mistake. He answered, "Yes?" and stopped in front of the group. There were five or six of them in denim jackets. An unmistakable gang look about them, clearly not killers, but definitely tormentors.

"I spit on queers like you," the one with thin black hair said. And true to his word he let loose with a gob that landed on the white sock of Billy's left foot.

"Oh," said Billy, then he turned and hurried away from their laughter. When he got around the corner, he peeled off the sock and threw it in the bushes.

Why was he thinking of spit, for goodness sake? He'd

been thinking of all manner of unpleasant things since he had gotten up this morning. Dog bites, sexually transmitted diseases, car accidents, and now spit.

Billy was a mailman for the Gramenton post office, zip code 18091, so he had plenty of time to think about things, pleasant and unpleasant. There was not a whole hell of a lot to his job. Once he learned a few of the tricks, like presorting the junk mail, how much to put in the bag and where, how to walk the streets depending on what the weather was like, and so on, his mental time was pretty much his own. This morning, however, he wished his job was more diverting.

Guilt. Guilt always nudged his thoughts toward disturbing psychological terrain. He was feeling guilty because last night he had awakened with a serious craving. It wasn't a craving that could be satisfied, like a sudden hankering for a glazed doughnut, or a bowl of Breyer's butter pecan ice cream. It was a craving of the physical sort, the lustful sort, which expressed its presence in a powerful erection. That would have been okay, because of course Billy was male, single, and subject to bouts of lust. But last night he had lusted for a particular woman, a particular *married* woman, a married woman who was his best friend's wife. This craving had caused his heart to flip-flop and the sweat to burst from his pores and drench the little hippos that embellished his favorite summer pajamas.

True enough, he had always had a thing for Nelly. And it was freely admitted, known to all concerned, casually acknowledged and dismissed by Max and Nelly, and even by Billy, as something safe and foolish. Billy's love for Nelly was treated as a sort of compliment, a statement of admiration, and nothing more. Max never felt threatened because nothing was ever meant to come of it, or could. But last night Billy was set tossing and turning in his narrow single bed by a perspective of Nelly that could only be called illicit. Billy had never even imagined holding hands with Nelly, so he was pretty shocked to be jarred from his sleep with sudden nocturnal yearnings of a rather provocative sexual nature. Wide-eyed and staring at the ceiling, Billy imagined Nelly standing above him in her angel-white nurse's uniform, smiling and calling to him in a low voice. Then she began to undo the buttons of her uniform one by one, slowly, revealing in bits of pink flesh that she was wearing nothing underneath.

Now, Billy was one of the few thirty-year-old innocents left in the world. He was not unfamiliar with women, certainly, but he was 100 percent unfamiliar with having lustful thoughts about his best friend's wife. All night long, Nelly came to him undressing and dressing, like the same movie shown forward then backward a hundred times. The little hippos on his pajamas were swimming in rivers of sweat by the end of the night.

So Billy stumbled along his route that morning, unrested and full of guilt, wondering what had brought Nelly into the bedroom of his imagination. He was inattentive to his work, which Mrs. Mentzner, scrambling after him and waving something in her hand, was quick to point out.

"This isn't my mail," she said thrusting a handful of envelopes at him. "What are you trying to do, put me in jail?"

Billy looked at her and pushed his cap to the back of his head. "Put you in jail?"

"Sure, sure," said Mrs. Mentzner. She had the sharp tiny eyes of a Chihuahua. Her tongue, too, moved in and out of her mouth in a pant. "If I had opened those letters, I would have been breaking a federal law."

"Why would you have opened them if your name wasn't on them?" said Billy mildly. He was afraid of this dog woman.

"Don't you get smart with me," she snarled. "I can turn you in for this."

Billy tipped his cap and turned away from her without a word. She had the temperament of one of the numerous dogs who tried to lunge through the screen door at him. His mere presence angered her. It was best to move on, let her growl and snap until she grew bored with it or until his scent drifted away.

* * *

Across town at the residence of Max and Nelly Lakeman, human communication was equally askew. Nelly was not quite snapping and growling at Max, but she was getting there. They had been home from Peleg's for a week now, and Max had gone through each day in some sort of funk. Nelly was getting tired of trying to draw him out.

"Look, Max," she said. "You're going to have to help me out a little here."

Max stared at her, then looked down at his feet.

"You say you're not sick, you say you're not depressed, you say it's not me, it's not you, it's not the children. You've said a lot about what it's not. Come on, honey, give me a clue."

"I'm just . . . nervous, I guess," Max said. "You know, just thinking too much."

"Okay, well, that tells me something, that narrows the problem so at least I know it's not physical. Now I know you don't have cancer or something." She came to him and hugged him from behind. "So what kind of nervous?"

It was an appropriate question because Max was given to many forms of nervousness. He was pretty good at fretting and worrying, too. There was nothing large or small that had not at one time or another caused at least a tiny acidy twinge in Max's gut. He worried about being an alien, or he worried about being the only human *surrounded* by aliens; he worried about rust on his mower blades. And he was nervous. Talking on the telephone made him nervous (it seemed unnatural to him that his voice became an electric impulse and then became a voice again when it hit the person's ear at the other end). Watching his children blithely attempt to scale a flight of stairs made him exceedingly nervous. And he fretted. He fretted from his bowl of Rice Krispies in the morning (how had the American public been beguiled into thinking that *snap-crackle-pop* was benign?) to the brushing of his teeth at night (how much toothpaste gets swallowed accidently in a lifetime?). Max was a sensitive man, a hypersensitive man in fact. His feelers were always out and sending to his brain more information in a day than most humans receive in a lifetime. And he carefully processed every piece of that information, devoting the same amount of serious thought to the minutiae of *snap-crackle-pop* as to the mighty questions of life, like: why in a world full of zinnias and Ingrid Bergman movies was there also evil in the hearts of men?

Despite all this mental handwringing, Max was a happy man. The zinnias and Ingrid Bergman movies molded his disposition to a greater degree than the existence of evil. So it was not like him to be in the doldrums for an entire week.

"What kind of nervous?" Max asked back. He fidgeted. The kind of nervousness caused by a beautiful woman rising from the waves or stepping out of his rhododendrons in the middle of the night. But he couldn't tell Nelly. He tried and tried, but it wouldn't come. Was she doing this, was the beautiful stranger causing the words to catch in his throat?

He knew from Nelly's dark look that he would have to give her more. "I don't know what it is. It's like this floating thing." Well, that was true. The woman did float on top of the waves. "Like a feeling that something's about to happen." He shrugged helplessly.

"You've got the dreads," said Nelly.

"The floating dreads," Max said with a little smile, his first in a week.

"Well, if you got to have them, that's the best kind to have, because eventually they just float away."

"Yeah?" said Max. She was talking to him the same way she did when she was quieting the night fears of Ben or Nora. It felt good. His nurse-wife knew just how to treat him. A little bit of that acidy feeling left his stomach.

Nelly did not press him for more. She had enough medical savvy to know when her patient was turning the corner, when to intervene and when to let the body, or the mind, heal itself.

* * *

Summer moved on in Gramenton. July with its three burners on high gave way to the four-burner month of August. Four burners plus the oven on 450. It was always a month of great suffering for Bilko. The days were so hot she hopped across the street like a rabbit, then collapsed in the shade to lick and examine the pads on her poor feet. At night Max could hear her roaming through the house in search of a pocket of coolness. She'd click down the halls, then click down the stairs to the kitchen to drop her tongue into her water bowl and pass out on the linoleum.

Heat and terror. Terror took the form of thunder and lightning. Bilko always gave them a half-hour warning before any thunderstorm. She would suddenly leap into the air as if the floor had come alive beneath her and goosed her. Then she'd stand stock-still, and her eyes would begin to bulge, her brown peepers rimmed with white. Her ears would slick back; she'd let loose with one bark of warning to the family, then slink off to the bathroom, where she would endure the fury of the storm, wrapped around the drainpipe of the sink. Max was reminded of jumping under his little wooden desk in elementary school during atom bomb drills. For poor Bilko, it was no drill—the atom bombs were actually falling.

If it was a particularly bad storm, Max would get under the sink with her and coo calm words at her.

"It's okay, come on now, it's okay."

A crash of thunder gave Bilko the distinct message that it was *not* okay. A flash of lightning underlined the message.

"I know it sounds pretty bad out there, but have you ever, once, been struck by lightning? In fact, I have heard of absolutely no case of a dog being struck by lightning. You're too low to the ground. Look at me, I'm a biped. I could get zapped at any moment. See, evolution is not always such a good thing."

But she was unable to appreciate his attempt to intellectualize the danger away. Her trembling brain could not comprehend anything but a landscape of flashing light and the boom of death. It took her about a half a day to regain her composure after a storm had passed. For hours afterward she'd be walking around, then suddenly she'd stop and sit, trembling, the aftershocks of dog fear working their way out of her body.

The rain, while no good for Bilko's psychological well-being, brought the lawns back to life, and Max was busy again walking happily behind his beloved machines. It had rained enough to make it look and feel like spring had come once more, at least in the morning before the heat began. The slant of the bright morning sun caused the grass to glow with that unnatural shimmering green of new growth. But by 10:00 A.M. and his third lawn, spring had disappeared, and Max tied his red bandana into a headband to catch the sweat that poured off him for the rest of the day. He didn't mind sweat. Sweat told him his body was working efficiently, a machine using its own fluids to adjust instantly to a changing environment. His mowers had no such capability, and Max monitored their juices and oils carefully. In return, they purred along gratefully, cutting the thickest, most unrelenting lawns for him.

He moved on to the next job, the Legland place. When he turned onto Guernsey Road, he saw Clement Strokas's battered truck. Clement was standing in a driveway giving hostile looks to a mower turned on its side. Mowers looked so helpless and off balance that way. Max shook his head and parked his pickup beneath the sycamore in front of Mrs. Legland's. Bilko leaped out and immediately began barking at Clement. Max had not seen her so worked up since the night she discovered the woman in the rhododendrons.

Clement was not in the mood to be barked at. If Max had not been around, he would have revved up his Weed Whacker and gone after Bilko. When he was done with Bilko, he'd pour gasoline on his mower and fry the shit awful piece of crap.

"Morning, Clement." Max waved to him as he came over to retrieve Bilko. "Get over here, girl."

Clement watched him in fuming silence.

"Funny how Bilko barks at you. You're the only one she does that to."

"Yeah, funny," said Clement. He took off his green work cap and dragged a sleeve across his heavy brow.

Max stared at the mower. It looked like an abused child, and when Max turned to him, Clement definitely looked like the guilty father.

"Yeah, well, the thing was a piece of crap to begin with," said Clement defensively. He hated Max for always making him feel somehow dirty. He couldn't understand why Max was not as miserable as he was. Mowing lawns for a bunch of rich fat fucks too lazy to do anything but reach into their wallets. Whenever Clement saw Max, he was smiling, smiling and pushing his lawn mower like it was a toy and he was three years old and didn't have a care in the world.

Clement and Max had been in high school together. Back then Clement had been smiling, too. Nothing mattered, things were easy, it was a good time. Being out a few years, though, wiped the smile right off Clement's face. He got lost in the transition, he never shook off his high school attitude of not giving a shit. Over the years it gathered momentum and lost him jobs, money, and soured his marriage. Before he knew it, he wound up behind a lawn mower, a job for losers, for guys who didn't have the wit or the balls to make it doing anything else.

So why didn't Max know he was a loser? Clement would drive by and see Max looking over a lawn, that goddamn dog sitting beside him, looking over a lawn like it *mattered*. Max cared. He really cared about his mowers, his edge trimmers. He even gave lawn tips to his customers like he was handing them news that would make them a million bucks on the stock market. His lawns looked like a million bucks, rich and green and full, every blade of grass glowing with vigor. Enough to piss you off if you were Clement and you felt chained to your lawn mower, if you knew the only reason you ever got a lawn contract was because Max was too busy to take it. Everyone in Gramenton tried to get Max and settled for Clement only if they were desperate enough.

Max bent over Clement's upended mower, examining it with a solicitous professional eye.

"Won't start?" said Max, running his hands over the machine.

What Clement really wanted to do was kick Max in the ass while his back was turned.

Instead, he gritted his teeth and said, "Yeah, well, Max, thanks, I can take care of it." Which was true. He was about to take care of it with a hammer. "It's the fuel line, keeps clogging up on me."

"Could be, could be," said Max. "But I don't think so."

Here it comes, thought Clement. Dr. Lawnmower and his magic diagnosis. He and Max had been going through this little routine for years, Max offering Clement advice he didn't want but needed, Clement pretending not to listen but following Max's suggestions as soon as Max disappeared. Max knew the routine, too; it was what drew the two of them together. He and Clement communicated by way of these injured machines, this link between their separate worlds. Max had a vision of reality, a special one, and so did Clement—askew and dark though it was.

"No, I don't think it's just your fuel line, although that may be part of it," said Max kindly, trying to give Clement some sense of control. He'd learned that from listening to Nelly. It was important to allow the patient input into his care.

"Look here," said Max pointing.

Clement followed Max's finger.

"It's your flywheel. One of the fins is a little bent. See? Right there."

Clement squinted. Jesus shitting Christ. How'd Max see that? That fin was just a hair off.

"Maybe you're right," said Clement. "I might check it out when I clean the fuel line." He jerked the mower back upright and started to move away from Max. "I can't stand here wasting time. I got lawns to do."

Max watched him go off.

"You know, Bilko," he said, "Clement Strokas is an asshole. It's too bad."

This was not news to Bilko. Someday she might bite Clement just for the hell of it, take a great big hunk out of his sour flesh.

Max went back to his pickup, put the ramps in place, and eased his big Bearcat down to the street. He started it up, listened a minute, then cut it off again. He got out his tool box, found the eight-millimeter socket for his metric wrench, and tightened the drive belt tension on the mower. Then he started it back up, listened again, and was satisfied.

First he did the back of the Legland place. It was a big lawn that should have been easy, but Mrs. Legland made things difficult by scattering odd-shaped flower beds and shrubs all over, so it was like cutting grass in a maze. It was a challenge, especially with the Bearcat, which could cut down a small tree if he lost control of it. He'd get the bulk of it with the Bearcat, then come in with the Toro and Weed Whacker to finish it.

He'd been mowing this lawn for years, and still Mrs. Legland came and sat in a lawn chair, watching him as he worked. She kept waiting for him to behead a petunia or gut one of her precious shrubs, but it never happened. Max didn't mind. Mrs. Legland was so old and peculiar he was amused by everything she did. She'd sit out there in her red sweater on days hot enough to cook a meatloaf, and crane her withered neck trying to keep up with Max. She couldn't see four feet past her nose, so Max could have run the Bearcat straight through her hybrid day lilies and she'd never have known. She'd pretend she could see, flapping and waving at Max (she'd locate him by the sound of the mower) and calling to him in her scratchy voice, "You watch out now. You keep away from my begonias." She didn't even have begonias anymore. Her gardener, Hayward Bemus, who came Monday and Friday, planted the beds with flowers he liked; Mrs. Legland was working with a memory of what her yard looked like when she could still see. "Mind now, keep that machine out of my bleeding hearts," she'd say, her eyes on a garden twenty years gone.

She thought Bilko was a cat. "Here, kitty," she said when Bilko appeared ghostlike in front of her. She squinted at Bilko, then at Max as he came to say good morning. He always did this and asked her permission to cut her lawn.

"Morning, Mrs. Legland. I'm here to cut your grass, if that's all right with you."

She considered this a minute, a queen bestowing favors.

"Well, I suppose if you must, you must," she sighed. Then her voice hardened and got extra scratchy. "But you stay away from my dahlias."

What dahlias? "I will, Mrs. Legland."

Bilko barked at a squirrel, and Mrs. Legland turned at the sound.

"Your cat's got hairballs," she said. She turned back to where Max had been standing, but he had moved to grab hold of Bilko. She spoke into empty space. "A man who won't take care of his cat's hairballs probably won't take care of my dahlias."

"I'll take care of both, I promise, Mrs. Legland. Well, I have to get started now."

When he finished the backyard, Max stopped for lunch. He sat beneath a sugar maple in the side yard, chewing on a tomato and cheese sandwich and drinking a Coke. He loved Coke even though he could practically feel the sugar turning the enamel of his teeth into mush. He wouldn't let Ben and Nora near the stuff, hiding his habit from them as if he was an alcoholic.

Nelly just shook her head when he drank one. "God, the

caffeine in that. . . . You can just kiss your heart good-bye."
He was always having to kiss some part of his body good-bye.
Pepperoni pizza—good-bye, arteries. Spaghetti sauce, for
God's sake—good-bye, stomach lining.

"Spaghetti sauce?" he said. "I thought tomatoes were
good for you."

"Sure, in low dose," said Nelly. She thought of things
in doses. "But spaghetti sauce concentrates the acid, and the
acid eats right through your stomach."

And she was always threatening him with colostomies.
"Sure, eat your Cheerios," she said to him in the mornings.
"They're great if you want to end up with a colostomy."

"I know for a fact that Cheerios is the world's most benign
cereal. If Cheerios are unsafe, if that's what you're telling me,
then the world has gone mad, and I'm going out to the barn
to shoot myself."

"We don't have a barn," Nelly said blithely. "Cheerios
don't provide bulk. You need to eat more bran, more fruit."

"Oh, Jesus," moaned Max. "You sound like a commercial."

"I sound," she said, "like a person who has had patients
with colostomies. And if they had taken care of themselves,
eaten a little bulk instead of Cheerios every morning, they
wouldn't have wound up with plastic bags taped over the holes
in their bellies."

"Don't," said Max. Nelly the nurse was only too willing
to play hardball. She was a compendium of human disaster
stories, and Max never stood a chance against her.

"Why can't we talk about something more pleasant," he
said.

"Like Raisin Bran?" she said.

Max downed the rest of his Coke, then leaned against the
maple. Bilko stretched and yawned beside him, showing her
soft jagged lips. She looked up sharply at the low rumble of
a jet, but it was not thunder, so she relaxed again. Max closed

his eyes and listened to the raspy sound of cicadas rising and falling in waves. It was the sound of summer, glorious summer. He half dozed, lulled by the heat, the insects, the smell of the freshly cut grass.

He came to slowly, opening his eyes as if waking from an enchanted sleep. First he heard the cicadas, then he smelled the grass again and smiled. And there was Bilko standing several feet in front of him, looking at something and wagging her tail. He watched her tail, a metronome ticking off dog joy. Then he looked up and beyond Bilko and focused on a woman leaning over the picket fence that bordered the Legland property. She was staring at him.

Max jumped up, scraping his back against the maple tree. He knew this woman, he knew her eyes, her hair, her smile. She was wearing clothes now, ordinary clothes, and there were no pelicans dropping flower petals, no music in the wind. But it was definitely our lady of the rhododendrons, the woman of the waves.

She spoke to him, her words shaped by an accent Max couldn't place. "You mow lawns?" she said.

Max replied, "Yes." He couldn't believe the woman was here, that he was talking to her.

"I'm new. My husband"—she paused and looked away ever so slightly, then met Max's eyes again—"my husband and I just bought this place."

She gazed past him. "Would you be able, do you think . . . ?" And now her voice took on a thickness, and she said the words slowly, her meaning unmistakable, "Would you mow my lawn?"

Bilko's tail stopped wagging. Now it was her head that moved back and forth, from the beautiful stranger to Max, from Max to the beautiful stranger.

· 5 ·

ONCE, unbeknownst to Max, Emmett had cheated on Doris. This would have shocked Max because he did not see his father as a passionate or frivolous man. He couldn't imagine him in the arms of another woman, couldn't think of Emmett without Doris, as if the two were actually one person. But there was a time, early on in his marriage to Doris, that the idea of staying with her for the rest of his life scared the pants off Emmett. It kind of came on him out of the blue. He had been on break with some of the train crew, and the engineer on the Patsburg line, an old guy of about fifty who was always spouting personal wisdoms, had something to say that morning about marriage.

"You know, marriage," he said, staring at the younger men with a sly look, "it's there when you want it, and it's there when you don't want it." Then he laughed that big, thumping laugh of his.

Emmett was the only one who wasn't laughing. He took off his blue conductor's cap and ran a nervous hand through his hair.

"What's the matter, Emmett?" said the engineer. He picked on Emmett because he was so quiet. "Don't you get it? There when you want it, there when you don't want it. Right, boys?"

Oh, Emmett got it all right, of all the young snickering

men crammed into that steamy back room, he was the one who really and truly got it. The engineer's little witticism precisely defined the vague sense of confinement that Emmett had been feeling over the last few months. He found himself waking at night and propping himself up on one elbow to stare at Doris. He listened to the thin whistling sound she always made as she breathed through her nose. In the dark, suffering from a nervousness of unknown origin, the whistling sound became for Emmett the high-pitched warning screech of a siren. Warning him of what? That he was married, forever, to a woman who made funny noises through her nose when she slept?

No, and yes. The fuzzy orange robe she wore at breakfast, the robe that he had once loved to feel when he hugged her in the mornings, now seemed ridiculous and clownlike. The orange robe, her uncombed hair, and scuffing slippers—he *had* married a clown.

She was not a clown. She was a fine woman, she had done nothing wrong, she tried to please him in every way. What was the trouble, then? Well, the engineer summed it up for him. Doris was there—when he wanted her and when he didn't. She exuded thereness. From her bathrobe in the morning to her whistling nose at night, Emmett knew just what to expect, as if he'd been married to Doris for fifty years instead of only two.

Emmett was not exactly of breathtaking interest himself. He too was a creature of odd and predictable habits, of dumb hats and funny noises. But where he could tolerate or overlook these deficiencies in himself, he was not so forgiving of Doris. He didn't know why. It made him feel rotten. It made him feel lonely. And it made him look at other women.

Being a conductor was the ideal job for a man who wanted to look at women. There were scads of them boarding the Patsburg local heading into Philadelphia every morning. They were mostly secretaries, bank tellers, department store clerks, the progenitors of the high-powered women who would alter the rules of the game in Max's time, but they were definitely not high powered themselves. They wore tiny hats and tight girdles, and some had on white gloves. Emmett never would have stood a chance in Max's time, but these women were an easier lot to get along with.

The gloomier he felt about Doris and the prospect of being married to her forever and ever and ever, the more desperately charming he became on those morning train rides. If Max could have boarded a time machine and seen his father moving down the aisle working those girdled beauties like a poolside Lothario—such silliness! Even Emmett in his agitated state could see that. But he was addicted to flirting now, and the engineer who teased Emmett for being so quiet shook his head and whispered knowingly to the rest of the crew.

Chattering and touching, down the aisle Emmett went, punching the women's tickets with a jaunty flick of his wrist. Inevitably, with the sheer number of women he came into contact with and the unceasing energy he put into it, someone responded to his call. Her name was Miriam Rodolfo, and she was a cashier in the young misses department at Wanamaker's. She boarded the Patsburg local at the Boothwyn stop. One morning when Emmett reached for her ticket, she pulled her hand back and smiled, and thus commenced a playful tug-of-war. When it happened, Emmett knew he had found his woman, his other woman. His heart pounded then, and each time they played the ticket game.

Emmett, in his panic not to wind up with Doris for eternity, had blinded himself to the fact that Miriam Rodolfo was not a spectacular woman. Had he been more sensible, had he calmly held side by side a photograph of each woman and listed their attributes, then slept on it for a night or two, he might not have fallen so readily for Miriam.

Perhaps Max, stepping out of his time machine and speaking rationally to his father, might have dissuaded him from cheating on Doris. Or the engineer, wise in the way of men, could have taken Emmett aside and said, "Son, keep it in your pants. Your pecker may not thank you, but I guarantee in the long run you'll be a happier man."

But no wise, responsible words were spoken to Emmett. He fell for Miriam Rodolfo, imagined in her the qualities of a goddess. She was no prettier than Doris, maybe even less so, no wittier, her clothes were not smarter. But she had something over Doris—she was someone else. The ticket game Emmett and Miriam played became more complicated and somehow more erotic. She began holding the stub closer and closer to her body, and Emmett would take a deep breath and reach for it, his fingers trembling with the prospect of what they might brush against. It was a good thing Miriam usually managed to find an unoccupied seat. But it soon became evident that that crowded train was not the proper setting for their fun times, and that's when the full-blown cheating-on-Doris period of Emmett's life began.

Emmett told Doris that the first and third Tuesday nights of every month were the meeting times of Local 109, the Brotherhood of Engineers, Conductors and Railmen. He told her he had been elected treasurer and that he had to attend the meetings. Doris never opened her mouth. Why should she? There was no reason to suspect her husband of anything. The 1950s were indeed a time of innocence.

Emmett, though he was a low-down and dirty wife cheater, was *not* a son of a bitch. That is, he was never unkind to Doris. He did not berate her, tell her to lose weight or dye her hair, or do any of the things a man dissatisfied with his wife might say or do. Doris went placidly about her end of the marriage. All went smoothly.

Emmett went to Miriam's every first and third Tuesday at 7:15 P.M. on the dot. In Miriam's small apartment there above the hardware store in unimpressive Boothwyn, Emmett was a man transformed. He spent his illicit hours hopping all over her, dancing, kissing. He was primal man unleashed. He said foolish things, he was gay. Miriam asked him no questions and he told her no lies. She didn't expect anything from this conductor. She knew that he would keep punching her ticket as long as she kept paying her fare.

Which was two years, and then it suddenly ended. The end had something to do with Miriam not paying her fare but had more to do with time. Time is very important to a conductor, or at least it used to be, and it was very important to Emmett. Being "on time" had a cosmic significance for him. When the Patsburg local was running on time, Emmett felt a spiritual glow; he was keeping pace with the universal ticktock.

One Tuesday evening at 7:15 P.M. on the dot, Emmett knocked on Miriam's door and she did not, as was her custom, immediately answer. He heard her scrambling around in the apartment, heard her say, "Oh, jeez, I didn't know it was so late." Emmett stood there more than a little irked, but the promise of things amorous quieted his chronologic disappointment. Who knew what sort of kittenish preparations had distracted her?

"Oh, Emmy," she said, half opening the door, "I'm running a little behind. If I let you in, will you promise not to look?"

"Sure, sure," he said. "Come on, don't be silly." He did not like standing outside her door whispering.

He would have been happier if he had stayed in the hallway, happier if he had kept his promise not to look. But he did, and what he saw was Miriam with her hair every which way, standing before him in a fuzzy orange bathrobe.

Emmett said one word, "Yikes." Then he said a few more. "Look, um, I'll come back, Miriam, I'll come back when you're ready."

He never did. Miriam in her orange robe was indistinguishable from Doris. What he saw standing in the doorway of that apartment was a bathrobe with two heads popping out of it, his lover's and his wife's. Emmett did the conventional thing—he went back to his wife and stayed there. He felt like a spanked child: hurt but wiser in the ways of the world. He learned a valuable but depressing lesson. Lovers, in the end, are not much different from your wife. So why not stick with the wife, who is really pretty nice and who, after all, got there first. Doris's nose whistling no longer distressed him, nor any of her other habits and ways. Emmett never strayed again, the young goddesses on the morning train no longer tempted him.

And he never saw Miriam again, although Boothwyn was only seven miles from Gramenton. She no longer boarded the 8:03 Patsburg local. When Emmett left her, Miriam wondered if it was because he somehow knew that she was pregnant. She had discovered this the same day she let him into the apartment for the last time. Being unwed and pregnant in 1954 was the kind of thing that made you lose track of time and open the door for your lover with your hair a mess, and wearing an orange bathrobe.

Things turned out all right in the end for Miriam. She soon married the Lithuanian baker whom she had sometimes dated, but never on first and third Tuesdays. Fortunately, math was not his strong point. Eight months, nine months, what difference? He was pleased that his young wife was so fertile and had so soon given him a son.

Nelly was having another fine day at Forkton Community Hospital. Nothing like short staffing in an intensive care unit to raise the fear quotient, to elevate the adrenalin to near toxic levels. Nelly stared at the two LPNs the nursing office had sent to work with her. One of them was looking around the unit bug-eyed—she'd never worked in intensive care before. She had the face of someone who has stepped into a hostile world, a world of strange machines and twisting tubes, of stink and unsavory death. She'd clearly be great in a crisis. The other nurse was older and her face told the opposite story. She was puffy with disinterest and boredom. In a crisis she'd probably tell you she couldn't help because she was on break.

Nelly was a veteran nurse and that made her feel confident, confident that she was about to have a disastrous eight hours. Report from night shift sounded like the reading of a casualty list from a war zone. Everyday life seemed to be a war there were so many victims. Nelly smiled once when she imagined Max listening to this report and looking around him. All his worst suspicions were confirmed here. There were eight patients, a full house, in the unit. Four were gorks on respirators, one was a young motorcycle accident, two were fresh MIs, one of whom's failing heart the night nurse called a "real mush job that could blow anytime—good luck." She smirked when she said that to Nelly, because the nurses thought of really sick patients as hot potatoes—you just try to keep the person alive until the next shift so you won't get stuck with the code, the paperwork, and the reeling family members. The last patient was a TBF, total body failure, in nursing lingo. It meant the poor man's entire structure was shot, his heart, kidneys, and lungs were shutting down, even his skin was covered with oozy sores. But he was alive thanks to catheters, needles, and IVs.

"All right, team," Nelly said stoically when report was over. "It's us against them." The bug-eyed nurse looked at her in near panic, the puffy one yawned.

"I don't think I can handle this," said Bug-eyed.

"Sure you can. It won't be that bad," said Nelly, stifling the urge to give her a good shake.

"I'll tell you one thing," said Puffy. "At 11:30 I go to lunch no matter what."

"Listen, folks," said Nelly. "Let's just do it, okay? We'll get through the day together." She nudged Puffy a little to one side and whispered harshly, "And I don't want a lot of shit from you today, you got that? You'll go to lunch if and when there's time."

And so it went. Nelly took meds and beds 4, 5, and 6— one gork, a fresh MI, and the old guy with no body left. She ran around all morning changing IVs and dressings, suctioning her respirator patient, helping the others turn and wash their patients. It all went pretty well as long as Nelly kept moving.

That was a trick she had learned long ago. Keep moving; even when you're caught up, don't stop—use that time to get ahead, to save time for the inevitable disaster, the sudden ER admission, the patient going bad on you.

At eleven she finally got to spend some time with bed 6, her old guy. She had saved him for last because although he was so sick, there was not a lot to be done for him except maintenance care. These types tended to get neglected when the unit was busy, and it made Nelly feel guilty.

She got everything ready to wash him and change his bed. His ancient face looked like an aerial photograph of rugged terrain, wrinkled and uneven, spots of brown, tufts of hair like trees. She bent over him and his eyes opened, two liquid craters stared up at her. It was a little spooky.

"Coot, coot," he said faintly.

"What's that, Mr. Ennis?" she said softly.

"Cooties," he said in a voice suddenly loud. Nelly jumped.

"Cooties?" She tried not to smile. She hadn't heard that word since elementary school.

"Don't touch me, I got cooties." His crater eyes waited for a reaction.

"You don't have cooties."

"No?" He shifted weakly. No heart, no lungs, no kidneys—she was surprised he could move at all. "Well, that's good to know, good to know. Then cooties are the only thing I ain't got." He laughed a little, and Nelly melted. This was her kind of patient.

She started to wash him, moving gently, trying not to hurt him.

"Can I ask you a question?" she said, threading his thin arms into a clean gown.

"Ask," said Mr. Ennis.

It was the question she often put to old people. "Does it feel like you've lived a long time? Does it go slow or fast, or what?"

He was quiet a moment, his eyes opening and closing slowly. "I got bad news for you," he said finally. "It's over in a minute."

Nelly sighed. They always, always said something like that.

"I know," he said. "It stinks." He was getting a little out of breath from talking. She put his nasal oxygen on.

"Is there anything I can do for you, anything I can get you?"

He turned his white head on the pillow. "Get me my wife, get me my mom and dad. I miss everybody." His voice was fading to a whisper. "I miss everybody and everything. I want my mom." His eyes were closed, and Nelly saw him mouthing *Mom, Mom* until he fell asleep.

Nelly stared at him and thought of Max lying there, Max as an old man. It was not his sort of thing, he would not do well. He will treat his failing body like a lawn mower, like one of his machines, and he will not understand that he cannot fix it. And he will miss the world just like Mr. Ennis, probably more. Nelly could hear Max calling out for Bilko, calling out for her. She hoped that she would be there.

After lunch, just when Nelly thought she was going to make it through the shift unscathed, the fresh MI started to go bad. She was watching the monitor at the front desk when his heart rate suddenly shot up to 140. She ran into his room, and the man was sitting bolt upright in bed, pale, sweating, and gasping for breath.

Nelly shouted from the bedside, "He's in failure, put a stat page in to Dr. Lawson!"

She turned up the oxygen and helped the man sit up. She heard the page come over the intercom just as an elegantly dressed man with thick eyebrows and curly gray hair stepped into the room.

"I'm sorry, sir, visiting hours . . ." she began. The man was very big, his features massive but beautifully proportioned.

"My dear woman," he said, speaking slowly but precisely, the words shaped by a strange accent. "I am with Dr. Lawson's group. I am new here. My name is Dr. Zeno."

"Hello," said Nelly, getting right to business as always. "My name is Nelly Lakeman, and this man's in failure."

"Yes. And he will soon be out of failure." He removed his white coat and draped it carefully across the back of a chair. He was wearing gold cufflinks in the shape of little lightning bolts.

"Please get eighty milligrams of IV Lasix. And four milligrams of morphine. I will attend to matters here." He took hold of the patient while Nelly rushed out of the room.

The other nurses came up to her. "Who is that doctor?" said the puffy nurse. She was fully awake now. "My God, he's good-looking. And big."

"I guess," said Nelly, getting the medications ready.

"You guess?" she said.

Nelly looked over her shoulder at the main monitor. As she watched, her patient's heart rate began to drop, 130, 100, until it hit 70 and stayed there.

Jesus, she thought. What's going on here? She hurried back into the room. Dr. Zeno was sitting on the edge of the bed, his long legs crossed, calmly talking to the patient. And the patient, no longer short of breath, his color good, was just as calmly nodding his head in reply.

Dr. Zeno turned to her. "Yes? You seem surprised." He smiled, his mouth full of white teeth.

Surprised was not the word for it. Nelly had seen many patients in heart failure, and never, ever, had she seen one of them come out of it spontaneously. If something wasn't done, Lasix, morphine, digoxin, rotating tourniquets, *something*, the person died.

"I don't understand," she said finally. "What did you do? Did you give him something?"

He just smiled. The patient watched the two of them, his head going back and forth.

"Why did you want me to get the Lasix and morphine?" she went on.

"I had you get them for *you*," he said. "So that you would feel useful in a way you understand."

"I'm afraid I don't understand at all," she said.

"Well, that is not important for now, dear Nurse Lakeman. What is important is that our Mr. Jameson here feels better. You feel better, yes, Mr. Jameson?"

"Yes," he said on cue.

"I must go now," said Dr. Zeno. He looked at Nelly, and for a moment their eyes held, then she had to turn away, flustered.

When Dr. Zeno was gone, Nelly asked Mr. Jameson, trying to sound reasonably casual, "What exactly did Dr. Zeno do? I was out of the room, so I didn't catch it all." Catch it all? She hadn't caught a goddamn thing.

"It's kind of strange. You know, I'm not really too sure," he said. "I was terrified. I felt like I was drowning, like the other night when it happened before."

Nelly had been on then. Mr. Jameson had to be loaded up with a lot of digoxin and Lasix before he finally came out of it. It took almost an hour.

"But this time, it was different," he said. "I couldn't really catch what he was doing and saying, because I was just trying to breathe. But he put his hand on my chest and kind of pushed or something. I'm not sure he said this—his accent's pretty thick and I was scared—but it was something like 'Lungs, breathe. Heart, beat.' Something like that. Whatever he did, it worked."

Heart, beat. Lungs, breathe. Nelly finished the shift in a daze. The other nurses thought she had had too heavy a dose of that dazzling Dr. Zeno. She'd had too heavy a dose, all right, but of what she wasn't sure.

6

NELLY and Max and Billy and Bilko sat in Nelly's and Max's backyard staring up at the night sky. Of the four of them, Bilko was the only one not distracted by disconcerting thoughts. In fact, Bilko was rarely troubled by *any* thoughts, which is one of the great benefits of being a dog. But the other three were squirming in their lawn chairs, looking for answers in the stars.

Nelly saw in the stars the brilliant eyes of Dr. Zeno. He had appeared a few more times, always in moments of crisis, when a patient was in real trouble. He never went on rounds or was on call, but he still knew all about the patients right down to their latest lab results and most recent X rays. Most of what he did for the patients were the usual sorts of things—the standard treatments and medications. But if there were no other nurses (except Nelly) or doctors in the room, and if the patient was in a particularly bad way, Dr. Zeno practiced a different sort of medicine.

With a woman who was bleeding internally, who had thrown up five emesis basins of blood, Dr. Zeno had finally dipped his forefinger in some of the blood and drawn a figure in dots on the woman's belly. She stopped bleeding instantly, her pressure and skin color soon returned to normal.

"But that's not possible," Nelly had said.

"Yes, it is possible," said Dr. Zeno. "But only you and I know it." That night he had been wearing a splendid white tuxedo as if he had just come from a grand ball. The red blood on his finger was his carnation.

"You're performing miracles," said Nelly uneasily. She was a nurse, and nurses *never* see miracles.

"No," he laughed. "I am simply healing in a manner you have never seen. It is unusual to you, but do not mistake what I do for miracles. I merely intervene."

"Who are you?" Nelly said.

"Dr. Zeno, a man so skilled in medicine the nurses believe he performs miracles." He smiled engagingly, as he wiped the blood from his finger.

"Not nurses. Nurse. I'm the only one who sees what you do. Why?"

"Who? What? Why? So many quesions. I cannot bear it." He winked, bowed to her, and disappeared down the gray hospital corridor. When she closed her eyes and sighed, she saw the dark negative of his white tuxedo, like the afterimage left by glancing at the sun.

Dr. Zeno, it seemed to Nelly, was up to many things. It was obvious, of course, that he was showing off and that his performances were meant specifically for her. With the rest of the hospital staff he was courteous, aloof, and proper. He did not intend to impress them. But he displayed his skills for Nelly. Which meant in some way she was special to him. His bow, his wink—was he playing, fooling around like doctors do? Dr. Zeno flirting? No, he was a man who didn't have to flirt. He was a man of direct intentions. If he could heal a wound or stop the flow of blood with a gesture, he could certainly approach a woman without bows and winks. His display, his performance then, was a message: I am very different and I have shown you only a very small portion of my powers.

Powers? Nelly shifted in her lawn chair. It was the sort of thing possible in Max's complicated world, but not in hers.

Until now. Perhaps Max was rubbing off on her, maybe she was seeing Dr. Zeno the way he would. The man was certainly exotic, and his ways were definitely peculiar, but did that mean he had *powers?* Max would say yes. For Max the white tuxedo alone would be incriminating. Nelly had not yet told Max about the tuxedo, or any of it, and she wondered why.

As she watched the sky, a group of stars above the line of maple trees began to shift and rearrange themselves, and the intensity of their glow increased. Her mouth opened but she did not speak. Billy and Max didn't seem to notice. Nelly stared at what the stars were making—a new constellation. The dots of light, she instantly realized, were a grand-scale version of the design Dr. Zeno had drawn on the bleeding woman's belly. Nelly hadn't recognized the figure then, because she'd been so flustered and Dr. Zeno had quickly wiped it off. But now, high above the maples, a great starry Z twinkled in the sky. And then it disappeared, as if erased by the unseen hand of the doctor in the white tuxedo. In an instant Nelly no longer wondered whether he had powers, but how he intended to use them.

Billy saw something quite different in the stars. In Boy Scouts he had learned to identify all the constellations for his astronomy merit badge. Tonight the heavens were less benign than they had been back in those innocent days. He used to imagine himself as Orion the hunter, bravely pursuing the mythical beasts of the night sky. Hunched now in his chair, staring glumly into the darkness, it was he who was being pursued. They were all after him; the constellation called Billy the Sinner was being chased by Scorpio, Taurus, Leo, Draco the Dragon, even Musca the Fly. Billy deserved to be caught, eaten by Leo, digested by Musca.

Just sitting next to Nelly put Billy in a fidget. His dreams about her had become so ridiculously carnal that when he actually saw her he was surprised she had her clothes on. And disappointed, which of course compounded his bountiful guilt. Freud would have loved Billy, the dreams, the yearnings, the guilt.

Tonight, when her arm brushed his while reaching for a hot dog, Billy nearly passed out. And reaching for a hot dog, for God's sake! She need not reach for a hot dog, his was close by. This crude thought made Billy blush all the way to his toes. Nelly looked at him, and he quickly stammered something about too much hot sauce on his nachos.

"You all right there?" she said to him.

"Yeah, I'm fine." He could feel the heat pulsing off his red face. Soon, his eyebrows would begin to crackle and smoke.

"Yeah, you look fine," she said dubiously. "Remind me not to eat the hot sauce."

"Tasted fine to me," said Max.

"I'm a wimp," said Billy. "What can I say?"

"Billy's a wimp," said Ben.

"Wimp," Nora repeated. "Wimp, wimp." The word felt good in her mouth. She said it again and again until Ben stepped behind her and put his hand across her mouth. She bit him, so he whacked her arm, then they both began to cry.

Max picked up Nora, and Nelly reached for Ben.

"Order in the court!" said Max. "Order in the court, the monkey wants to speak. No more hitting!" He frowned at Ben.

"She bit me," he whined.

"And no biting," he made a face at Nora. She managed a grin through her tears.

"Wimp," she said again.

"Oooh, you're evil. You just can't help it. You got the

evil in your soul. Where's your soul? Where's your soul?" He tickled her belly, searching for her soul.

"So, Billy," Max said later when Nora was safely asleep in her playpen and Ben was off tracking down crickets (the fireflies of early summer had disappeared). "How's the female situation?"

Billy felt the red creeping into his face again. "Well, um, the girl of my dreams has yet to show up." Did he just say that? He was really asking for it.

The girl of his dreams, who was less than two feet away from him, said, "Come on, Billy, you haven't troubled us with your sex life for weeks now."

If Nelly wanted trouble, she just had to read his mind. He was remembering the dream he had last night. She was the sexy nurse, and he was the patient requiring special treatment, like in one of those movies.

"I'm kind of off love for a while," he said.

"Summer slow you down?"

"Yeah, well, I guess." He sighed. "It's pretty discouraging."

"You'll find somebody. Everybody does."

"Not true. Ugly people, for instance, have a hell of a time."

"Ugly people find other ugly people," Nelly said unconvincingly.

"Oh, great," said Billy. "The birds-of-a-feather theory. I'm a skinny mailman. That mean I'm going to wind up with another skinny mailman?"

"Mailwoman," said Nelly.

"As a matter of fact," said Max, "we had a new woman deliver our mail last week. Wavy brown hair, nice looking?"

"Great. Marla Henderson. She doesn't know a postcard from a first-class letter. The woman has no mind. Took her two weeks to learn the Gramenton zip code."

"So she's not a postal genius."

"Also, she happens to be married. I don't make the moves on married women," he added emphatically.

Billy looked up at his constellations. He wished he was a Boy Scout again, he wished he was Orion. He caught Nelly's scent when the night wind picked up, and wished he was Max.

What was in the stars for Max? Oddly, he was the least troubled of the three stargazers. He could feel something was up with Billy, and with Nelly, but he didn't ask what. He meant to, but he listened instead to a voice murmuring in his ear. The voice was beautiful and soothing, and it told him to be still, not to worry.

The voice belonged to the woman at the picket fence.

"Would you mow my lawn?" she had said.

Max had been unable to answer at first. All he could think was, there she is, there she is. She's here. It was like having Santa Claus and the Easter Bunny walk into his childhood room and say, "The truth of the matter is, Max, we're *real*. Now what can we do for you?"

She leaned on that fence as real as can be. She did not fade away into the swirling mists or sprout the wings of a dove and ascend into the clouds. The wraparound skirt she wore was from Strawbridge's, he was sure, because he had bought one like it a month ago for Nelly's birthday. The cotton top, too, was a style Max had seen the women wear this summer. The costume was right, it was daylight, the woman had spoken to him. It was his turn to speak to her, to complete this initial contact.

He opened his mouth to speak, but it was old Mrs. Legland's voice he heard.

"Max, where are you, Max? You still here?" Mrs. Legland was making her semiblind way to the front yard, bumping into things, like Mr. Magoo.

"Over here, Mrs. Legland!" Max called, then went over to her. She'd never have made it on her own.

"I didn't hear your machine," she said, yanking her arm away from him. Mrs. Legland did not like assistance.

"I was eating lunch."

"Lunch?" She squinted at him. "How do you mow my grass and eat lunch at the same time?"

"Well, I don't. I stop mowing—"

"Exactly. You stop mowing. This is not a union job, young man."

A classic Legland line. She was crafty and wonderfully mean spirited. "Mrs. Legland," he said, "you have a new neighbor." He turned her toward the fence. "I'd like you to meet . . ." But there was no one there.

"What?" said Mrs. Legland. "What did you say?"

"Your new neighbor, she was here a minute ago." Why was she always disappearing?

"My new neighbor? I have a new neighbor? What happened to those snots the Simpsons?"

"They moved, don't you remember? They put the house up for sale."

"Moved? Well, hallelujah. Their damn cats were always chewing on my parsley. Not like your cat, you've got a well-behaved one."

Bilko looked up at her.

When he got back to his pickup, there was a note on the front seat. It was written on scented paper. It read:

My apologies for leaving so abruptly. Would Thursdays after lunch be a good time for you? I will expect you unless you tell me otherwise.

—Mrs. Zeno

He did not see the words "cut grass" or "mow" or "lawn care." He was not surprised. He held the note to his nose a moment, then ripped it into tiny pieces. Thursdays. Thursdays were pretty busy, but he figured he could fit Mrs. Zeno in somewhere after lunch. He could have fit her in if she wanted him Sundays at three-thirty in the morning—who was he kidding?

That was a week ago, and now he sat in the backyard with his wife and his best friend under a canopy of stars on the eve of his imminent indiscretion. These last few days he had felt swept along by the inevitability of what he was about to do. He felt as powerless as a child. A woman, a veritable goddess, was pursuing him. She had appeared before him in a diaphanous robe in the rhododendrons; she had risen naked from the sea and beckoned him with her finger.

He was supposed to resist a woman like that?

Nelly, as if reading his thoughts, reached in the darkness for his hand. Her eyes were closed, her face faintly lit by a distant light. Max looked at her. She had never risen out of the sea for him or dressed in diaphanous robes. It was not her style.

Max had never cheated on Nelly. Their marriage was a stable statistic in a world of 50 percent divorce rates and rampant adultery. He had been tempted, certainly, but had never succumbed.

There was that woman over on Lafayette Avenue he used to work for, Lois Stafford. Lois was about ten years older than Max, attractive in a pinched, urgent way, and she wore clothes designed for nubile teenagers. Max used to have to brace himself for the costume she'd be wearing when he went to the door for his weekly check. She insisted on giving him a weekly check, even though Max explained to her that most of his customers paid monthly, or in full at the end of the season. No, no, it had to be weekly, it was her way of keeping "on top of things." She almost giggled herself right out of her pink tank top when she said it.

One day when he went to the door, she appeared in a black body suit and a white miniskirt. She looked like a piece of pop art from a retrospective display of the sixties.

"Max," she said in a voice so breathy he could feel the moist wind on his face. "I'm afraid I don't quite have your check ready."

"That's okay, Mrs. Stafford," Max said. "I'll get it next time."

"Oh, no, I couldn't do that to you. Please come in. It will only take a minute."

What, Mrs. Stafford, Max thought, would only take a minute? A minute for you to get "on top of things"?

Max was kind, he didn't run away and make the woman feel foolish. Besides, she was interesting to look at, as bizarrely clad as she was. She had fine breasts and a fine bottom, which were the assets successfully emphasized by all of her clothes. So he stepped into the cool dark, which was a mistake. Inside the house those breasts and that bottom made Max instantly nervous. They reminded him that there was a husband to be considered, and quite possibly a husband who was insanely possessive of his wife's flesh.

Max followed her into the kitchen, where, to his great distress, Lois turned her back to him and began to peel the body suit from her shoulders. To her right, on the kitchen table, lay his weekly check.

For all Max knew, sitting now in the dark holding Nelly's hand, the check was still there. He turned and ran; he did not want the money, and he did not want to see Lois Stafford's bared breasts.

Why not? Because he was a coward and because he didn't want to cheat on Nelly. Those two truths had kept him straight for ten years of marriage.

He liked being married; he liked being a grown-up, a daddy with two children, a wife, a house. If you cheated on your wife, they took all that away from you. These big black moving vans with faceless drivers pulled up in front of your house, and they loaded up the marriage, the kids, the dog, the shrubbery, all of it, and left you sitting on the curb in your emotional underwear. And the underwear was not very clean.

Fact. Nelly did not deserve to be cheated on.

Fact. He never had.

Fact. He was an ordinary man, with a tendency toward good behavior.

Fact. An extraordinary temptation had arisen.

Mrs. Zeno was not Lois Stafford. Mrs. Zeno was not Fay Mosby.

Fay Mosby was a former girl friend of Billy's, known to Max and Nelly as "The Toucher." Billy would bring Fay over to the house, or the four of them would go out together, and Fay would spend the entire time touching Max. She couldn't speak to him without putting her hand on his arm, his shoulder, his leg. His leg. Max couldn't understand it. How could you place your hand on a person's leg when you talked to them?

And Fay did not so much talk as she did coo. Her voice went all soft and sticky when she spoke to Max. It was bizarre. Her conversational tone was perfectly normal with Billy and Nelly, but when she turned to Max, hand reaching out, her resonance changed.

"Boy, you must really have the pheromones," Nelly had said.

"I just don't get it." Max was mortified for Billy. But Billy seemed nonplussed by it all.

"There's nothing to get. You simply exude chemicals, and poor Fay is helpless."

"Poor Fay! Poor Fay is trying to pick me up right in front of her boy friend and my wife."

"The woman is a victim, a moth drawn, blindly if you will, to your light." Nelly thought the whole thing was pretty funny.

But Max wasn't tempted. Here was a perfectly attractive, though definitely peculiar, woman, and he wasn't tempted. He could have had a bit of a fling; he could have put his hand on *her* leg and cooed right back, "Okay, Fay, enough with the warm-ups already, let's play ball!" But he kept his hands in his pockets and the one-liners to himself.

Fay, like all of Billy's women, eventually disappeared. They were supposed to go with Max and Nelly to a movie, but at the appointed hour only Billy showed up.

"Where's your date?" said Nelly.

"My date will be permanently late," said Billy. "She is now my ex-date."

"You exed her, huh?" said Max, relieved.

"Oh well, just one of those things. She had bad habits, you know."

"Did she?" said Max.

"Yeah. I'd take her to the museum and she'd touch the paintings. I'd take her to the supermarket and she'd touch the asparagus. I'd take her to my best friend's house and she'd touch my best friend."

"Whoops," said Max.

"Bad habits. A disruptive influence. You weren't having fun, I wasn't having fun. So I gave her the boot."

Nelly clapped her hands and Billy bowed.

He said, "You know what her last words to me were? 'Say good-bye to Max for me, will you?' "

"Oooh, that woman had to go," said Nelly.

Max just looked at Billy. "She said that? She really said that?"

Lois Stafford, Fay Mosby. There had been others, too. Over the years, temptation in forms big and little had knocked repeatedly on Max's door. But he had not answered. The temptation of nice women met at parties, the amiable chats poolside at the swim club, the wives home alone while he ran his mower back and forth before their picture windows. Max never took a situation farther than safety and good sense allowed. He was a coward, he was an ordinary man. He loved Nelly, he loved his children, his life. He did not want the faceless movers to park their black vans in front of his house.

But. But Mrs. Zeno had risen naked from the sea. And her voice came to him now, disguised as wind in the trees, hidden in the sweet night chirping of the crickets. Max held Nelly's hand there in the backyard beneath the stars, listening to another woman's voice.

Summer was coming to an end. Max lived for summer. The heat warmed his blood and his heart. He sat in the dark reminiscing about this past summer, his thoughts for a moment turning away from the inevitability of Mrs. Zeno. He remembered Ben and Nora with their shirts off standing beneath the glittering spray from a garden hose, the drops of water like falling jewels. He remembered walking in the sun each morning, inspecting his yard, his garden, to see what had grown and what had finally died. He thought of sitting on the front porch steps watching the neighbors, waving to friends driving by in cars, his friends waving tanned arms back. And of watching Bilko yesterday, the way she ambled from spot to spot, from sun to shade, sun to shade. The way she rolled on her back, kicking her legs toward the cloudless sky in a seizure of pure joy. He thought of all the lawns he had cut over the past months, all the different types of grass, the hidden roots, the perfect sound of his mowers, well oiled, the metal hot and clean. And Nelly. Nelly in the sun, her long brown hair in a single thick braid, Nelly licking barbecue sauce off the tip of her finger. Nelly holding his hand in the dark, Nelly torturing him with postmortems of her days at the hospital, Nelly lying in bed on a hot summer night, the fan breeze carrying her scent as she talked to him in her calm reliable voice, in a voice known to him, known to him.

And then the siren sound of Mrs. Zeno reached him again, and he had to listen. The sound said, Come to me, Max. It was the sound of summer coming to an end.

7

*S*UMMER coming to an end suited Clement Strokas just fine. Goddamn summer. By the end of the season he was so tormented by the repetitive stupidity of cutting grass, so plagued by fickle fucking lawn mowers breaking down on him, so sick of customers, *especially* Mrs. Leston, he was ready to hang himself. Or better yet, here's what he'd do. Clement leaned against the battered door of his truck smoking a cigarette. What he'd do was juice up his biggest mower—the self-propelled sucker that chewed everything it hit, rocks, baseballs, a box turtle Clement hadn't really meant to run over—he'd juice it and go right up Mrs. Leston's front walk with the beast, nailing her impatiens all the way. When she came out, he'd just hop the mower up onto her porch, push it through her front door, and let that baby go. He could just see it, Mrs. Leston screaming and jumping around, and that mower eating through her living room, chewing rugs, chewing furniture, crashing around in her dining room, her kitchen. Serve her right.

Mrs. Leston just had to watch, just had to give advice. Like it took a lot of brains to mow a lawn. He'd be going along cutting the grass, and she'd appear at the edge of his vision, flapping her arms and yelling something he couldn't hear and knew he didn't *need* to hear. But he'd have to cut the engine and go over to her, because she was the customer.

"What'd you say, Mrs. Leston?" He'd stand there looking at the ground because he could not look the woman in the face. She looked like Miss Beety, his third-grade teacher. Same yellowish hair, same fat red nose, same voice squawking commands.

"I said, you're cutting too close to my zinnia bed. You got one of my prize Giant Reds."

Clement saw the spewed red remains of the zinnia. The red looked good splattered on the green.

"Didn't see it, Mrs. Leston."

"How could you possibly miss it?"

"Didn't see it, Mrs. Leston." Fuck you, Mrs. Leston.

She glared at him. Then she said, "And how about over there, Clement, those brown patches near the pine?"

"What about them, Mrs. Leston?" Jesus H. Christ.

"Well, you're the professional, aren't you?" she said, oozing sarcasm.

He looked her in the face for the first time, raised his death ray eyes slowly until they bored straight into Mrs. Leston's baby blues. She blinked, then she blinked again and stepped back ever so slightly. Clement stared at her awhile longer, then turned and walked back to his mower. When Mrs. Leston hurried back inside, he sideswiped her asters and smiled as the blue shreds shot across the lawn.

Back at the truck now, he smoked his cigarette. He could see Mrs. Leston at the edge of her picture window peeking through the curtain. He stubbed the butt against the door of his truck, threw it onto the freshly mowed lawn, and got into his truck to go home for lunch.

Clement's family life was like Max's viewed in a distorting mirror. The home in Gramenton was there, the house, the wife, even the two kids. But something was off. There was no pleasure in any of it for Clement. Where Max reveled in domesticity, Clement was tormented by it. It seemed to him his home life was as broken down and guaranteed to aggravate as his mowers.

When he pulled into his driveway, he smoked another cigarette in the front seat of his truck. Then he got out, walked in the front door, and said the same thing he had said for the past seven years.

"Yo, babe, I'm home."

His wife, his babe, in his La-Z-Boy chair flipping through a magazine, didn't look up. Then again, Clement didn't look down as he went past her on his way into the kitchen. Why should he bother? This small troll with thin brown hair cut in no discernible style, this tiny woman with the greenish pallor was not news to him.

"Bologna and cheese," she said, in anticipation of the inevitable question from Clement.

"Yeah?" he said. "You must have busted your butt to fix that."

"You don't like it, you fix something else." He heard her throw her magazine down and stomp up the stairs.

Clement stared a moment at his bologna and cheese sandwich. There it sat, as stale and uninteresting as his life. He bit into the sandwich and it tasted of marriage, of hot stinking lawns, of children bickering now in the backyard.

He dragged himself from the table and went over to the open window. Out on the lawn his two small boys tumbled furiously on the grass. He was about to open his mouth, then decided against it and sat back down at the table. In front of him on the refrigerator door there was a photograph of him and Linda, his green-skinned wife, on their wedding day. Both of them had been smiling, but you couldn't see Clement's smile anymore because there was a brown food smudge on the picture.

Clement's smile was gone and it had been gone for years. There was nothing in this kitchen that made him happy; it gave him no sense of home, *his* kitchen. He may as well have been in a diner, a bad diner that served bad bologna sandwiches. The kids in the backyard were not his kids, the pouting wife upstairs could not possibly be his wife. He wished, just for a moment, that Max could fix it all for him. Fix the wife, the kids—Max would fix his life, as he fixed his battered mowers. Dr. Lawnmower and his magic touch. See, Max might say, pointing to a place on Clement's wife, recognizing the problem as if it was as simple and obvious as a slightly bent blade on a mower. You just adjust it like this, he'd say, and *poof*, Mr. and Mrs. Clement Strokas would be in one another's arms again, smiling like newlyweds. And *poof*, the kids fixed, too, and then the four of them would be together, the happiest family on the block. Maybe they'd even get together with Max's family, barbecue in the backyard, kids running all around. . . .

Clement swallowed hard, the last bite of his sandwich catching in his throat. Ah, fuck, listen to me. Best thing would just be to let the big mower go in *this* place, he thought, dropping his plate in the sink, next to the plate off which he had eaten yesterday's sandwich. Rev up that big son of a bitch and push it in the door one day, and then just get back in my truck and *go*.

Instead, Clement got back in his truck and went off to his next job. He picked up his clipboard. Thursday afternoons, he had to do the McWilliamses' yard over on Guernsey Road.

When he got there, he saw Max's blue pickup pulled in front of the big white house that had been for sale a few weeks back. Clement smacked the steering wheel—Max had stolen another lawn from him. Truth was, Clement knew Max could have taken any of his customers any time he felt like it.

Clement stopped under the shade of a sycamore and sat watching from a distance as Max went back and forth over the grass. He could see that Max's lips were pursed, that he was whistling, whistling while he worked like one of the seven dwarfs. And there was his goddamn dog on the sidewalk watching him.

And then an interesting thing happened. A woman Clement had never seen before, it must have been the new owner, opened the door to the side screened porch and stood there for the longest time watching Max. Snow White? Max didn't see her, at least not at first. Suddenly, he slowed his mower and turned and said something to the dog. The woman, who'd been watching all this time, raised an arm and pointed at Max's back, and as soon as she did that, Max whirled around and faced her. Like she was sending him some kind of message or zapping him or something.

Clement quick lit another cigarette, hunching over to hide the flame. They stood there for a while, the woman in the doorway, Max with one hand on his mower. Finally the woman began to move toward Max, and Max moved toward the woman, the sway of their bodies as perfect as a dance. Clement opened his mouth a little, the cigarette dangling on his lower lip. And then the clincher. When they got to each other, the woman held out her hand, and Max took it! Max took her hand, and the two of them walked back to the screen porch and stepped inside out of view. The dog ran to the door and scratched furiously, but no one let it in.

Clement felt a little giddy, something he had not felt in a long, long time, and never with less than a six-pack in him. Well, well, what do you know? What dooo you know? Max Lakeman, Mr. Pure, Mr. Good, Mr. Happy Marriage himself, was a man after nooky just like the rest of us. Max was getting it, how do you like that? Clement liked it. He whacked the dashboard and laughed. Was this Max's first time out, or did he do this sort of thing on a regular basis? Well, he was a caught man now, and Clement savored every moment of it.

"Hot dog," he said. "Shit," he said. Then he whacked the dashboard and laughed again.

The morning of Max's fall from grace was hot and sunny. The perfect day for cheating on your wife. Max had spent all night in the Church of the Scary Jesus Christ. His mouth had the ashy taste of guilt and remorse—guilt and remorse before the fact. The waxy-skinned Christs with their rolling, agonized eyes had tried to persuade him not to do it. If you do it, you will *join us, join us*, they chanted. It was a pretty forceful performance, with lots of blood and closeups of the wounds. But the Church of the Scary Jesus Christ was just Max's guilty imagination at work and was only useful in blocking smaller indiscretions. It was ineffective against the siren call of Mrs. Zeno. There were times during the night when he almost woke Nelly and told her, the waxy Christs almost got him to confess his desires. He'd reach across the bed to touch her shoulder, but then could not. He opened his mouth to speak, but the words weren't there.

So Max greeted the new morning in the manner of a storm-tossed sailor washing up on an alien shore—he had arrived, and there was not a whole hell of a lot he could do about it. He rose and, like the sailor, quiet and resigned, readied himself for a tour of a very unfamiliar island.

Max turned and looked down at his wife's sleeping form. His *wife*. Finally he spoke, awakened her from her sleep and watched as she opened her innocent eyes and took in the new day. Max suddenly rushed over and kissed her, then moved quickly away for fear she would taste something bitter on his lips.

"Mmmm," she said. "Where are you going so fast? Come back here."

"No time, no time," he said, hurrying into the bathroom. "I hear the little beasties waking up in their rooms."

"The beasties," she said, sitting on the side of the bed. She could hear Ben playing with Nora in Nora's room. "What was life like before the beasties, do you remember?"

"We were young," Max shouted from the bathroom, his words garbled by sadness and toothpaste. "Young and gay and free."

Ben came running into their bedroom at the sound of their voices and leaped on his mother.

"Umph," she said. "And good morning to you."

He jumped off the bed and charged into the bathroom and wrapped himself around his father's legs.

Max looked down at Ben's curly head. "Good morning, o firstborn."

"What's firstborn?" Ben said.

"You are. You were born before Nora, so that makes you firstborn."

"Oh," said Ben.

Nelly went and got Nora, then came back and deposited her on the bed. Ben ran from his father to join in. Max closed the door to just a crack and spied on his family. He watched as Nelly tickled Nora; he watched Ben tickle Nelly; he watched as they laughed and carried on in their happy fashion. Then he closed the bathroom door all the way and looked into the toilet, his hand clutching the towel rack for support.

Max stepped out the back door into the bright, hot morning. It did not seem like fall was coming, with this heat, and the grass still growing fast. But the signs were there, the brown edges on the sycamore's leaves, the dogwoods hinting at red. Max refused to look, he kept his eyes on the grass.

"Hey, Bilko, what do you think about today?"

Bilko stretched in the sun and wagged her tail. He reached down and gave her a long body scratch. She was in heaven, absolute doggy heaven. Distracted, Bilko didn't see the Pinkley's Dalmatian sniffing around down by the azaleas. Max did.

"Uh-oh," he said to Bilko.

Bilko looked at him.

"Oh, my God," he said.

Bilko stared hard at him, trying to pick up on what was wrong. She had not yet seen the Dalmatian.

"Lord, have mercy!" cried Max. "We're being invaded from the south." Finally Bilko caught on and whipped around 180 degrees. Max loved this part—the tensing canine body, the lifted fur, the throaty growl—Bilko on red alert.

The Dalmatian, meanwhile, looked up and saw Bilko preparing for a total ground assault. The poor dog's eyes showed fear, regret, and panic. It cowered, it wagged its tail, it would have waved a white flag if it had had one, but Bilko would not be dissuaded. She let out a war bark and tore down the yard after the intruder. The Dalmatian yipped once, then leapt over the azalea and took off.

Max loaded up his pickup to the sounds of Bilko's victorious after-barks. She was at her bravest when the enemy made a hasty retreat, and the Pinkley's Dalmatian, she had found over the years, was her kind of enemy. When Max started the pickup, Bilko came running and jumped into the front seat. She did this every morning, and it was either the perfect truck commercial or the perfect dog food commercial, Max couldn't decide which. As he pulled out the driveway, Nelly came out to the front steps in her orange bathrobe and bare feet and waved good-bye to him.

The second lawn of the morning was Mrs. Parkland's, with her towering oaks and JFK collection. With Max's imagination as busy as it was lately, JFK soon materialized in his customary place behind the yews.

"Morning, Max," said JFK. He was wearing a blue tie dotted with the Harvard insignia.

"Good morning, Mr. President—I mean, Jack." Max cut the mower and peered into the yews.

"You're, uh, looking a little white around the gills."

"Well, I've had a lot on my mind lately." Max sighed.

"So I've heard," said JFK.

"You have?"

"Sure, sure. Word gets around pretty quick up here."

"Even Walt Disney knows?" Max said. He didn't like to think Uncle Walt knew anything about adultery. Mickey Mouse had never cheated on Minnie.

"I'm afraid so, Max. And he's, uh, none too pleased, let me tell you."

"He's not?" Max was shaken.

"Don't worry about it, though. Disney's a prude. Nobody likes him."

"Jack, listen, I have kind of a delicate question to ask you."

"The answer is yes. Too many times to count," said JFK.

"Did Jackie ever find out, did she know, do you think?"

"She knew, she knew. They always know."

"Why did you do it?"

"For the usual reasons, Max. Now listen." JFK stood up straight and jabbed his finger just like he used to do at the press conferences. "I have, uh, some advice for you, some serious advice. . . ."

But Mrs. Parkland suddenly appeared with a glass of lemonade for Max, and JFK and his advice disappeared. The glass had a likeness of JFK etched on it, with the numbers "1917–1963" beneath. Max hid the numbers with his hand.

"He was our greatest president," said Mrs. Parkland, in the reverent tone of a believer.

"Oh, I know," said Max.

"I think it's just terrible, those stories you read in the magazines now. I don't believe them for one minute."

"Which stories are those, Mrs. Parkland?" Max drank his lemonade.

Through the other side of the glass he saw JFK's eyes staring at him.

"That trash about him and Marilyn Monroe, and all the rest of it." Mrs. Parkland shook her head in disgust.

The eyes on Max's glass did a Groucho Marx roll as he finished off the lemonade.

All through the morning Mrs. Zeno reminded Max that this was the day she expected him to come to her. At one of his jobs over on Amherst Avenue he was mowing next to a privet hedge when he saw something white, a piece of cloth, hanging in the branches. It was a bit of Mrs. Zeno's robe, the one she had been wearing the first night she had appeared. When he reached for it, the cloth vanished, leaving behind a hint of sea air. And at the Boyers' place, he was mowing along when Bilko suddenly ran in front of him and snatched something out of the grass with her teeth. At first Max thought it was a mole or something, which would have been a first, because he had never seen Bilko catch anything. Maybe it was a bone. Max cornered her and pried the object out of her mouth. Bilko, as expected, was reluctant to relinquish her booty, coating it with an extra dose of dog spit to get back at him. What Max pulled out of her mouth was not a bone, but a blue shell, a scallop shell. He looked over and saw Bilko lift her nose into the air and sniff. He lifted his and sniffed, too, and smelled the sea again.

After lunch, he did Mrs. Legland's place, his last lawn before Mrs. Zeno, right next door. Being so close to Mrs. Zeno was a distraction, to say the least, and Max had a great deal of difficulty concentrating on Mrs. Legland's lawn.

Mrs. Legland sat blindly in her lawn chair furiously tapping one of her canes. Something sounded wrong; Max was not cutting the grass in the usual way.

"What's going on out there?" she shouted, but Max didn't hear her.

Finally she was unable to stand it any longer. She got up out of the chair and weaved down the yard to where Max was working on the grass beneath the cedars. She was within whacking distance with her cane, was actually reaching out to give him a good one, when at last he looked up and saw her. He cut the engine.

"What's wrong, Mrs. Legland?" He had forgotten that he was even doing her lawn, his thoughts drifting over to the next yard.

"You tell me, Max Lakeman. What's wrong with you today?"

At first he did not understand, then he looked past her and saw. For the last half hour he had been cutting the grass in a crazy pattern. At first it looked like an endless series of zigzags, interconnected lightning bolts. Then, as if one of the lightning bolts had flashed in his brain, Max understood what he had drawn on the grass with the blades of the mower. Z's, he had filled Mrs. Legland's huge backyard with dozens and dozens of Z's.

"I'm sorry, Mrs. Legland. I wasn't thinking," Max said.

She regarded him with her cloudy eyes. "I'm not paying you to think, young man, I'm paying you to cut grass. If I had wanted a thinker, I'd have hired your cat here to cut my grass."

Bilko barked, and Mrs. Legland looked blindly in her direction.

"Haven't you taken care of that poor animal's hairballs yet? What am I going to do with you, Max? You're slipping in a big way, it seems to me."

In bigger ways than she could possibly imagine. Max cut the rest of the grass, erasing the Z's as he went along. When he finished, when the last blade of grass had been cut, there was nothing more between him and Mrs. Zeno. He went slowly back to his pickup to fill the mower with more gas before going around the picket fence into Mrs. Zeno's yard. "I will expect you Thursday after lunch," her note had read. It was Thursday, it was after lunch, he was expected.

But what did she expect him to do? The note gave him no instructions. He certainly was not going to amble on up to her front door and say, "Here I am." Besides—and now Max looked furtively up and down the street—he didn't want to be obvious about it. He didn't want to get caught. The thought made him dizzy.

Finally he decided to just go ahead and cut her lawn and see where that led. Besides, mowing gave him comfort and assurance.

And so, with Bilko in tow, Max Lakeman, happily married father of two, mower of lawns, stepped into the world of Mrs. Zeno. When his foot touched that first little patch of grass, he felt, or thought he felt, a tingle of electricity dance across the top of his work shoe and up his leg.

The house stood in the center of the lawn, pure white, a large Greek-revival mansion, with a portico of four columns. It was the right place for Mrs. Zeno. Max took a deep breath and reached down for the pull cord on his mower. He barely touched the cord when the mower suddenly kicked to life and started to move slowly off without him. Max froze as the machine moved down the yard, straight toward a rose bed. He ran after it but knew he would not reach it in time. He winced at what should have been the moment of disaster, but instead of plowing through the roses, the mower turned neatly and trimmed around the bed. When Max caught up with it and placed his hands on the handle, another tingle of electricity, like the one that went from the grass to his toes, shot up his arms.

The mower had a will of its own. Max felt as if he were holding the leash of a dog that knew precisely where it wanted to go, and he could do little but follow. He began to play a game. He rested his fingertips on the handle and let the machine work its magic, occasionally pushing it closer to roots and rocks than it wanted to go. Max was the master of precision lawn cutting, and the mower soon learned to accept his guidance. The machine and the man took their respective turns at the helm. Max began to whistle an aimless little tune. The sun shone brightly. Bilko was nearby. Max forgot the world, was completely alone with his magic mower, which sprayed an emerald arc of cut grass across the lawn.

And then he began to feel something strange right in the middle of his back. He shrugged. A bug crawling inside his shirt? No. It was more of a pressure, a sense of someone about to touch him. He stopped the mower, turned, and looked up. She was there. Mrs. Zeno stood in the doorway of her side porch pointing at him. It was her finger he had felt on his back. She had touched him without touching him. She slowly lowered her arm and smiled.

Max listened to himself breathing, listened to his heart beating in his ears. Was it really his lungs he heard, his heart? He seemed for a moment to be outside his body, watching it, watching Mrs. Zeno, seeing all perspectives, her and himself, simultaneously. His body began to move, and he returned to it. From across the way, Mrs. Zeno began to move too, her body in perfect rhythmic harmony with his own. As she approached, Max took in the entirety of her shining reddish hair, her sea-green eyes, her lips, her arms and hands.

She reached for him; she held out her hand as she had held it out when she had appeared in the rhododendrons, and again in the ocean waves. And now Max took it. At the instant his fingers touched hers, the effect was felt all over Gramenton.

Billy, delivering mail over three miles away, felt a sharp burning on the palm of his right hand and, thinking he was being stung by a bee, threw the mail he had been holding straight up into the air. Bees petrified Billy. But when he examined his palm, there was nothing there, and there were no bees in sight, only the scattered mail fluttering to the ground.

Emmett was in his house painting a window sash at that same moment and thought he heard a woman's voice, Miriam Rodolfo's voice calling to him. He turned, and as he did, he bumped the window, which came down on his fingers. He cried out, more in surprise than in pain. Doris, who was downstairs frying chicken, was startled and knocked into the hot pan. Searing drops of grease splattered on her hand, one of them large enough to cause quite a nasty burn.

Clement was burned too, but not enough to really bother him. When Max and Mrs. Zeno touched, he had been so intent on watching, he forgot he was holding a cigarette. It burned down to his fingertips, and that caught his attention. "Shit," he said, and lit another.

At day-care, Nora got a splinter in her little hand from the seesaw. At elementary school Ben fell on the playground and scraped his palms on the gravel.

Nelly received more than a scrape, more than a small burn or splinter. She had been helping a doctor with the insertion of a temporary pacemaker. When the doctor held out the scalpel for her to put on the instrument tray, Nelly wasn't paying attention. She was watching the patient's heart monitor. Where there should have been a tracing of the patient's heartbeat on the screen, a woman's face suddenly appeared. It was a beautiful face, and the woman had long brown hair. Then the screen returned to normal, and the doctor called Nelly's name again.

"Nelly, would you please take this scalpel and hand me the hemostats."

She reached for the scalpel, but still dazed from the face on the screen, she took it without thinking. The scalpel slashed into her hand between the index finger and the thumb. Nelly spent the next forty-five minutes in the emergency room getting stitched up. She had been a nurse long enough to know that when the wound healed, there would be a scar she would carry for the rest of her life.

Not even Bilko went unscathed. As Max held the hand of Mrs. Zeno, Bilko stepped on a thorn. She immediately sat in the grass licking her paw and trying to get at the thorn with her teeth. Why wasn't Max helping? When Bilko looked up from her self-ministrations, she saw Max and the woman disappearing into the house. Bilko raced after them, ignoring the pain in her paw, but she was too late. Although she scratched furiously at the door, no one let her in.

Max left Mrs. Zeno's house with the baffled morning look of a man who had just awakened and was trying to remember a complicated dream. What had happened in there? his perplexed face said. Bilko ran up to him and then stopped dead in her tracks. Max's scent was different—there was something new on him.

Max got into his pickup and sat. He stared at himself in

the rearview mirror. In the corner of the mirror, just disappearing out of sight, was Clement Strokas's battered truck, but Max did not see it. Staring back out from the mirror were the nervous eyes of a man who had just cheated on his wife.

But not in the usual way. Max sat in his pickup piecing together his encounter with Mrs. Zeno. He remembered taking her hand and letting her lead him into the house. When he touched her, he had a feeling of being thrown back to the first time he had touched a girl, to his primal erotic encounter. He had only held the girl's hand, just as with Mrs. Zeno, but he was overwhelmed by the intense novelty of contact, skin to skin. His entire body went erect and alert—he had become a walking phallus. His whole world became pleasurable, and he the perfect instrument to enjoy it.

He let her lead him into the living room. The room was white and very large, with high windows, a white marble floor with a stone column in each corner, and on the center of the floor, a pallet and two cushions. Nothing more. There was nowhere to go but to the pallet. Mrs. Zeno sat and pulled Max down beside her.

She was dressed in a white diaphanous robe, the one she had been wearing the first night. Max could see the outline of her body, the sun behind her highlighting her breasts and shoulders. She pulled back the robe a little, so that he might see more. Then she took his hand in both of hers and placed it just above her left breast.

With his hand resting there, Max looked for an instant up and out of one of the high windows that bordered the room. He could see the branches of an oak, the green leaves quivering in the wind. Abruptly all the leaves turned brown and dropped simultaneously from the limbs, so that the tree was part of a desolate winter landscape. He blinked, and the green leaves reappeared.

"Do not worry," Mrs. Zeno whispered, as the winter vision clouded his face.

Max pulled his hand away, and the spot on Mrs. Zeno's body where it had rested glowed, as if illuminated by an unseen source of light. He stared, then looked around him.

"No," she said, smiling. "You have done that. Your touch does that to me." She sighed.

Her sigh was a message of longing that Max could not resist. He leaned slowly toward her and kissed her on the lips. Her lips began to glow too, and so did the spot behind her ear he grazed with his fingers.

Mrs. Zeno let the robe fall from her; then kneeling on the pallet, she undressed Max. For a moment he stared at his brown, grass-stained work clothes, a pile of reality in the unreal white room of an unreal woman. Mrs. Zeno turned his face to her, then pulled him down to the pallet.

They made love. They made love enthusiastically, at times acrobatically. The pallet seemed hardly big enough to contain their flamboyant release. Mrs. Zeno did things to Max, then Max did things to Mrs. Zeno. They laughed and cavorted, playing without fatigue for a very long time until at last they could play no more. Empty, drained, and sweaty, Max rolled away from his magic partner. He absently let his hand fall on her hip, then pulled it quickly away. Mrs. Zeno was very hot. Now her entire body began to glow—her teeth and eyes sparkled, the strands of her loose hair radiated like the tails of a thousand tiny comets, her skin became too dazzling to look upon. And then, ablaze, Mrs. Zeno's long body slowly lifted from the pallet, rose a few feet, and hovered in the air. Max had to look away, to *move* away, the radiance from this woman was so great. In time she began to cool—at least that's how it seemed to him—and as she did, her body came to rest once more on the pallet. She sighed and went up on her elbow gazing at Max, who stood now against one of the white walls of the room.

"You satisfy me," she said.

Satisfy? The woman had been on fire! And though his own skin did not ignite, he certainly felt the flames, the fever of immoderate passion. He peered down at his penis, which if not actually scorched by excess, certainly looked small and weary.

"I will bring some iced tea to cool your thirst," Mrs. Zeno said, rising. She began to put on her robe, then stopped. "Would you rather I leave it off?"

"No, no," said Max. "That's okay." He started across the room for his own pile of clothes. "I'm sorry, I really can't stay."

"Why must you go?"

"Well, it's late. I have to get home." He thought of his pickup sitting out front all this time, a neon sign advertising his illicit presence. Jesus.

"Yes, I suppose. My husband will be coming home soon, too."

Husband. Max nearly dropped to his knees. Husband. What sort of man would be married to a woman like Mrs. Zeno? Yikes. He scrambled into his clothes.

Mrs. Zeno laughed. "Oh, do not rush about so. You have not been discovered." She kissed him and he was instantly calm.

He stood before her fully dressed. His shirt seemed tight, his pants too long—clothes felt wrong in this room.

He was suddenly shy. "We'll do this again?"

"Yes, Max." Her face was close to his. "We'll do it again and again and again." They both smiled.

But he needed specifics, some sort of order, a schedule. After all, there was Nelly, his family to work around, his job to consider. He wished he could come anytime, to throw off his uncomfortable clothes and roll about on the pallet.

With his lover. He was a married man with a lover now. He swallowed. Mrs. Zeno kissed him again and his thoughts came back to her. She would not let him stray. She would hold him captive with her kisses.

He licked his lips where her lips had been. "Thursdays? How about Thursday afternoons?"

She answered him with a kiss.

They walked, arms around each other, to the door. Max paused and looked into the eyes of his beautiful lover.

"Why me?"

"Because you wanted me so much."

"I don't understand."

"Someone like me could only happen to someone like you."

He started to speak again and she gave him a final kiss. "I am here, and for now that is enough."

Max stepped out of the white house and was immediately greeted by a very anxious Bilko who came running across the lawn to him. He had forgotten about her. In the soft arms of Mrs. Zeno he had forgotten everything. For an instant he wanted to turn around and go back.

Bilko reached him and jumped about sniffing at him, searching for clues to his long disappearance. She found them on his crotch and pushed her nose there for a deeper investigation. She was not pleased with the evidence.

"Down. Get away from there, Bilko." If Nelly's sense of smell was as keen as Bilko's, he was in trouble.

He'd have to take a shower as soon as he got home. And his pickup truck—he certainly couldn't take a chance leaving it out here every Thursday for two hours. A sour taste came up from the back of his throat. He didn't like this part of it, worrying about showers, hiding his truck. He licked his lips and tasted Mrs. Zeno, and the worry vanished, borne away on a green wave of desire and expectation.

"Come on, girl, get in, time to go." Max patted the passenger side of the seat, coaxing Bilko in. She jumped into the truck reluctantly and ignored him the entire trip home.

When he pulled into the driveway, Ben came running out of the house to give him the news.

"Daddy, guess what?" he said.

Max hugged him and said, "I can't guess, you tell me."

"Mommy's got a bandage!" A bandage was the kind of thing little boys took great interest in and secretly wanted for themselves. Bandages meant danger and mystery.

It certainly meant that to Max. "What do you mean, what kind of bandage?" Bandage had instantly escalated to body cast in his mind.

"He means this," said Nelly. She stood on the front porch steps holding up her right hand. It was wrapped round and round in gauze. Another vision of whiteness in a very white day.

He ran up the steps to her, Ben scurrying behind him. Ben knew something large had occurred, and he was pleased to be the first to report it to his father.

"What happened?" Max imagined beneath the bandage a mangled hand, fingers missing. You go off to meet your lover and here's what happens.

"Easy, easy," Nelly said, kissing him, but holding her hand out of harm's way. "It's just a cut. Well, a big cut. I reached for a scalpel without looking."

Max winced. He hated wounds, accidents. "Stitches?"

"Eleven. Want to see?"

He backed away.

"I want to see!" said Ben, pushing past Max.

"Our little ghoul," Max said, grabbing him from behind.

"So, Daddy," said Nelly. "Ain't no cooking tonight. Do we get to go out to eat?"

"You'll do anything for a free meal," he said, embracing her carefully.

"Yay, we're going out to eat," Ben shouted. What a day—eating out, his mother's hand in a big bandage!

Max showered first, washing gingerly between his legs, the soap stinging his tender, overindulged parts. He wondered whether he could physically tolerate more than one encounter a week with Mrs. Zeno. At the thought of her, his penis rose gamely, then fell again—the flesh weak, the spirit strong.

He got out, dried himself, and hurried into the bedroom

to help Nelly into her dress. She was having a time with her hand.

"Let me get that." He helped her get the dress down over her head. He looked at her body and was ashamed he did not want it more.

"Thanks. Could you get the zipper, too?"

The four of them headed off to The Fish House, Nelly's favorite. He didn't really like seafood, and generous Nelly tried to talk him out of it.

"Hey, listen," he said. "This is your night to howl."

"I howled already this afternoon in the emergency room."

"Right. So now you get a reward for being such a brave girl."

"Okay. You talked me into it."

They settled into a booth near the back of the restaurant. Max pushed the cracker bowl and the sugar packets beyond Nora's reach and helped Ben order.

"I want the lobster tail," Ben said.

They went through this every time—Ben knew all his lines. He looked up at his father.

"Nope," said Max.

"You always say nope," he whined.

"You always ask for lobster."

"Why can't I have it?"

"Because it is very expensive. Now order something else."

"Are we poor?" said Ben, refusing defeat.

"No we are not poor, Benjamin, and you can't have lobster, and if you don't choose something else by the time I count to five—one, two—"

"Fried shrimp!" he squealed, fried shrimp being what he had wanted anyway.

Max looked for the least fishy thing on the menu.

"Why don't you try the flounder? That's usually pretty benign," said Nelly.

"Nah, all dem little bones." He was afraid of fish bones.

They were translucent and evil looking, made for catching in the throat.

"Max. They debone it."

"Sure, that's what they tell you. Think I'll just go for a bowl of clam chowder and a salad." No bones, though the thought of ground-up clam's feet, intestines, noses, God knew what all, didn't much appeal to him, either. When the soup came, he swallowed all the unidentifiable parts like pills. He'd have held his nose, too, if no one else had been around.

Nelly watched him, smiling and shaking her head.

"Soup good?" she said.

"Mmmm, boy," said Max.

"If it's any help, I don't think they actually use clams in the clam chowder. Too expensive."

"Do tell?" He eyed the chunky liquid in his spoon.

"Yeah. I understand they use squid."

He let his spoon drop into the bowl. "You're a riot. How about the salad? Anything you want to tell me about the salad?"

"Salad's reasonably safe. Keep your eye on those chick peas, though."

That night Max sat on the side of the bed a minute before turning out the light.

"You okay?" Nelly reached over with her good hand and touched his back.

"I don't know. I felt a little weird, kind of woozy there for a second."

"Something you ate?"

"Very funny," he said. Probably was, though. Felt like a school of squid channeling through his intestines. Then a hotter, nastier feeling lower down in his belly.

He got up, went into the bathroom, and opened the medicine cabinet. An old bottle of Pepto-Bismol sat on the shelf. Its pink contents looked remarkably unsoothing. He braced himself and took a swig, then another, then rinsed his mouth and spat in the sink. The sight of his pink frothy spit did his nausea no good.

"Never again," he said, climbing back in to bed next to Nelly.

"Seafood? I told you you didn't have to."

"No, Pepto-Bismol."

"It's candy medicine anyway. We never use it at the hospital."

"Please, I beg of you, don't tell me what you do for stomachaches at the hospital. I don't think I could stand it."

At 3:00 A.M. Nelly told Max what they did for stomachaches at the hospital. His Pepto-Bismol pain had by then escalated to emergency room pain. He woke up at two and began to moan and twist in the bed. By three he was in the fetal position and yelped mightily when Nelly gave his belly a gentle prod. Bilko came up to his side of the bed and stood at worried attention.

"Christ, I'm dying," he said.

"Come on, sweetie, I'm taking you to the hospital."

"No, please." He was petrified. He knew too much about Nelly's place of business.

"Max, it's your appendix. It has to be. We have to go."

She dialed the phone and got hold of Emmett and Doris. Max viewed the world through a bubble of pain and fear—the walls seemed misshapen and close, Nelly's voice was distant, her words coming fast, then slow. She helped him into a robe, which was no easy task since he could not really unfold his body, and she had only one hand to work with. By the time she led him down the stairs, step by agonizing step, Emmett and Doris had arrived.

"Max, you don't look so good," said Doris, getting right to the heart of things. Emmett looked at his son uneasily.

"I don't feel so good, either," Max grunted.

"Doris, could you stay with the kids?" said Nelly. "They're still asleep."

"Hey, what happened to you?" said Emmett, seeing Nelly's hand.

"Long story," she said. "Could you drive us to the hospital?"

"You guys must have some kind of curse on you, or something," he said in a limp attempt to lighten things.

Max groaned as a particularly hot flash of pain cut into his abdomen.

The emergency room doctor at Forkton Community Hospital confirmed Nelly's diagnosis.

"Yep, that baby has to come out right now."

The words Max never wanted to hear. Well, you cheat on your wife, those are the words you deserve to hear. Max lay crumpled on the stretcher looking at the green tiles, smelling the sweet, scary antiseptics in the air around him, listening to the babble of medical voices, thinking of his imminent death on the operating table.

How would it come? He knew all of Nelly's horror stories. Most likely some sleepy anesthesiologist, too tired and pissed off about being awakened at 4:00 A.M., would overdose him, administer the Big Sleep. Maybe the surgeon would nick a vessel—Nelly said that happened—and he would slowly bleed out. Or his heart would stop. Somebody would pick up the wrong vial or give him a wrong dose, and his surprised heart would stop midbeat, filled with blood destined to go no further than those four dead chambers.

On the green tiled walls, crucifixes began to appear, the crucifixes of the Church of the Scary Jesus Christ. This was the perfect setting for them, this holding place before death. One green and bloody Jesus winked at him and leered. Max let out a cry.

A hand reached out and smoothed his sweaty hair.

"Nelly," he said.

"No, it's me," Emmett stood over him with a shaky smile. "Nelly's in the other room talking to the doctors."

"Dad?" Max was dreamy with pain. "Is my head okay?"

Another time Emmett had been there. Max had been very small and had fallen down the back porch steps and banged his head on the handle of the water faucet. Emmett appeared instantly, was right there scooping him up in his arms. Max remembered the feel of his father searching through his hair for the bump. It was a lovely, gentle sensation. Little Max had asked, "Is my head okay?"

Emmett did not try to figure out now what Max meant. He simply gave him the comfort he sought. "Yeah, your head's fine," he said, and ran his hand through his son's hair again, thinking how much time had passed since he had done such a thing.

Nelly came hurrying back into the room. "We're in luck. Dr. Rider is the surgeon on call, and he's good."

"Do I have to?" Max asked feebly.

"Don't be afraid, sweetie. I know that sounds dumb, but you're going to be okay, really." She leaned down and kissed him twice on the cheek, then held his hand.

Nelly, too, was afraid, in the way all insiders in the medical world are when someone they love becomes a patient. She knew the risks, but she was calm in a way Max could never be, Max whose imagination turned small risks into a sentence of death. She was sorry she had told him so much about hospitals.

The orderly came to prep Max's belly for the operation.

"How's it going, my man?" The orderly was a thin black guy with a shiny head. "Not so good, right?"

"Not so good," Max grunted.

"I got to put some of this brown antiseptic shit on you, make you clean. It's cold, watch out now."

The antiseptic was very cold, but it felt good on his hot skin.

The orderly looked down and smiled.

"You're scared, right? Think you going to die, right?"

"Right," said Max. He didn't think it, he *knew* it.

"Let me tell you something. I been here fifteen years, and

I painted a lot of bellies with this here shit." He leaned his shaved head close. "Well, me and this magic shit ain't never lost nobody. That's the record. One hundred percent down the line, that's right." He laughed in glee, then lowered his voice.

"Tell you something else. I'm afraid of your wife. She's good but she's tough. I let you die, she kick my black ass up one end of the hospital and down the other."

The anesthesiologist came in next, a big smile on his face.

"So, you're Nelly's husband. Glad to meet you, I'm Allen James. Nelly told me to tell you that I've had plenty of sleep, and that I'll be bright eyed and bushy tailed throughout your operation. I'm a night person, 4:00 A.M. is the perfect time for me."

Bushy tailed. Max tried to smile.

"Okay, Nelly gave me most of the poop I need to know. You have no drug allergies, right? Have you taken any medications in the last twenty-four hours?"

"I had some Pepto-Bismol."

"Right," he said without looking up from the chart. "No medications in the last twenty-four hours."

He rose to go. "So, I'll see you in a few minutes. A nurse will be in to give you a shot."

As he went through the doorway, Max thought he saw him yawn.

Nelly came back in with another nurse. "This is Lisa. She's going to give you a shot." The two of them helped him turn, and Max felt a ball of pain in the right side of his ass.

"I guarantee things are about to improve," said Nelly. "When that shot hits, you'll enter paradise."

Paradise. Was that like heaven? Max wondered. Would Walt Disney be there?

"Tell me one more time that I'm not going to die," he said, his words beginning to slur with the drug.

"Max, you're going to live forever."

They wheeled him down a corridor and into an elevator,

then down another longer corridor. They stopped the stretcher in front of a big pair of white doors. A huge man in green scrubs pushed through the doors. Max felt Nelly's hand tighten on his shoulder.

"Dr. Zeno!"

Max heard with unmistakable clarity the name, looked up at the curly-haired giant gazing down at him, and instantly passed out.

"But I thought Dr. Rider was the surgeon," Nelly said, her voice stretched thin.

"Dr. Rider called me and asked me to cover. He is unwell." Dr. Zeno looked into her eyes.

She drew closer to Max, who lay unconscious on the stretcher. She did not want Dr. Zeno near him.

"I want a regular doctor."

"Dear Nelly, I am the only surgeon here."

Max groaned. He was very white.

"Why are you always showing up? Who are you?"

He placed his hand on Max's belly. "Right now I am a surgeon, and I will tell you this. If I do not operate on him now, his appendix will burst, and we will have to deal with peritonitis."

Nelly believed him, because there was no choice. She grabbed Dr. Zeno's arm as he turned to follow Max's stretcher into the operating room.

"He's my husband, you know."

"Yes, I know." He looked at her again with those unrevealing eyes. "I, too, am married."

Max came to briefly as they eased him on to the operating table. "Hey there," said the anesthesiologist, from the top of the table. "You'll be asleep in a second, and then before you know it, you'll wake up in your room."

Max turned his head to see if the curly-headed giant was there, then the anesthesia took hold. Dr. Zeno followed him into his drug dream. The scrub nurse, the anesthesiologist, and the surgical assistant suddenly had walked out of the operating room, leaving him alone with Dr. Zeno. The huge doctor filled the room, his eyes as big as jack-o'-lanterns, his teeth king-size bars of Ivory soap.

"Well, well," Dr. Zeno said, his words loud against a background of menacing laughter. "So you're the little man who mows my wife's lawn."

Max couldn't move. He was pinned on the operating table. "She made me, she made me!" His voice was a squeal.

"Made you, huh? You know what I do with lawn-mowing little men?"

He pulled a chair up to the table and held up a knife in one hand and a fork in the other. "I EAT THEM!"

Max screamed as Dr. Zeno plunged the fork deep into his belly and began slicing with the knife, his monstrous guffaws echoing off the tile walls of the operating room.

Max screamed again and opened his eyes. Nelly? He was in a different room now, and Nelly was there.

"Hey, hey. Come on now. You're all right," she said, stroking his arm. "It's over, Max, you're okay."

"Dr. Zeno?" Max's eyes were wide.

"He did the surgery. He said it went well." When Dr. Zeno, in his green scrubs, looking tall and splendid, said those words, Nelly had suddenly wrapped her arms around him. They stood that way for a long moment until Nelly stepped back and looked shyly away. She had embraced him in gratitude, but also, she realized, to hold him, to hold another man. When she looked into his eyes, she saw that Dr. Zeno understood this, had even expected it. She looked away again, then turned to leave him—she knew how vulnerable grateful wives were to the charms of doctors, how vulnerable nurses were to surgeons with godlike skills.

Later, when he had slept off his anesthesia, Nelly told Max there had been a slight problem. His appendix had a small ulceration that leaked a little pus into his abdominal cavity. Dr. Zeno had to make a somewhat longer incision than normal so he could do some cleaning.

"So you didn't die, Max. See, I kept my promise."

"No, I didn't, did I?" Which seemed remarkable, since the man whose wife he was sleeping with had such a wonderful opportunity to do a number on him.

The next day, when the surgical assistant came by to take off the dressing, Max, screwing up his courage to look at his wound, saw that Dr. Zeno had done not a number on him but a letter. There on his right side, just above his transgressing penis (which the scalpel-wielding doctor had for some reason spared), was the letter Z carved into his flesh and held together by small silver staples.

Max went pale. "It's a Z," he said.

The surgical assistant looked up from cleaning the wound. "What?"

"It's in the shape of a Z." He was a marked man.

"A Z?" The surgical assistant studied the incision. "I don't see what you mean. It's the usual, it doesn't look like anything."

"Not a Z?"

The surgical assistant shrugged. "It doesn't look like anything."

It was three weeks before Max could push a lawn mower again. The first Thursday was red, filled with weakness and fatigue, and flashes of hot pain. He did not, of course, go to Mrs. Zeno. Toward the end of that day a dove came and fluttered outside his window, but he did not see it. The next Thursday was purple, the color of longing and desire. The dove came again and sat cooing outside his window as the sun went down. Max listened, hearing the sounds Mrs. Zeno had made when they were together on the pallet. He went to the window, opened it, and the dove flew to him and perched, light as a kiss, on his finger. A tear fell from the dove's left eye onto Max's hand. Then it flew out the open window.

The third Thursday was white, the white of Mrs. Zeno and her room. Max's wound was healing, and the ominous Z, if it had been there at all, began to disappear into healthy pink flesh. Max wanted Mrs. Zeno again very badly. It was Thursday, it was time to go to her.

It was fall now. Max wore a light jacket as he stepped out the back door and into the morning sun. He walked around his yard and studied, as he always did, the grass. It still grew, but more slowly now, and there were thin spots. Two or three weeks and the season would be over. He was about to start loading up his pickup when he stopped, turned, and looked down the yard at the rhododendrons. The early morning sun was behind them, throwing off long, sad shadows. As he moved his startled eyes back and forth, he saw that every tree and bush around him cast its own dark shadow on the lawn.

· 8 ·

*A*LL the secret longings of Max and Billy, the yearnings of Nelly and Emmett, their indiscretions, their fantasies, would have been beyond the comprehension of Doris Lakeman had she known about them. Doris was someone who still had the capacity to be shocked. Sex, in all its extramarital forms, shocked her. She was not a prude, exactly, but a woman who believed in the set of rules and moral conditions espoused during her prenuptial prime. Her mother, *Redbook* and *Woman's Day*, her friends, had all imparted the same information—there is a Mr. Right, and after you find him, there will never, ever be anyone else.

Mr. Right was Emmett Lakeman, whom Doris met in 1948 at a roadside fruit stand outside of Gramenton. Every so often, in the years that followed, Doris would say to Max or Fred or to a friend, "Women don't meet men at fruit stands anymore, do they?" She said this with a sort of misty longing, as if fruit stands had once played a significant role as a place of romantic encounter for America's postwar youth.

Emmett had been reaching for a cluster of grapes, and Doris a banana, and somehow their hands touched; there was confusion and shy smiles.

"You go ahead," Emmett had said.

"No, you," said Doris. "No really, you go ahead."

Gallantly, Emmett reached for the bananas and held out

an entire bunch to Doris. Doris beamed and took them, though really she had wanted only one. Then she reached for the grapes, giddy with the boldness of such an act, and handed them to Emmett. They both laughed, looked away, and laughed again.

Long after they were married, Doris would lie in bed at night, her stomach doing nervous turns. What if, what if there were no such things as bananas, or no such things as grapes —I would never have met Emmett. What if I had filled Mama's car with gasoline before I went to the fruit stand like she told me to—I would never have met Emmett. The "what if's" were about the most terrible things Doris could imagine. The "what if's" might have come between her and Mr. Right, of whom there was only one, now and forever.

If Max got his imagination, at least in part, from Emmett, who could see magic in the glow of fireflies, then he got his love for the day-to-day stuff of marriage from Doris. When she rose in the morning, she couldn't wait for Emmett to open his eyes. Such eyes! And then at night she couldn't wait for those eyes to close, because he looked so beautiful when he slept. The way Mr. Right stirred his coffee, checked the tilt of his conductor's hat in the mirror—it was more than she could bear. She was so happy, day after day, meal after meal, one ordinary moment after another with Emmett.

Even sex with him was a source of joy. Doris did have to admit to herself, though, that the sex thing was at first doubtful. Her mother, friends, and the various magazines of the time, all were imprecise and delicate when it came to providing certain specifics. Like what in the world do you do with Mr. Right's honeymoon penis? As it turned out, the honeymoon penis was not up to a performance on the big night. Emmett, who was not really a drinker, had had three and a half glasses of pink champagne at the reception. He barely got his tuxedo pants off before falling fast asleep on the wide hotel bed. While other women might have been just a bit put out, Doris was relieved. Having Emmett out cold beside her gave her a chance to take one step at a time, to experience things slowly. After all, she had never even been in bed with a man before. So while Emmett slept, Doris curled up beside him in her nightgown. After she got used to that, she took off her nightgown and lay naked beside her man. She even touched him, gently, in a few places. By morning Doris was pretty familiar with Emmett, so that when he awakened, sheepishly, and had had his shower, she was ready and willing to consummate their marriage. They did pretty well, for beginners, and for Doris it only got better.

Once she met Emmett, she never looked at another man, and once she married and made love to him, she knew she would never—even if he God forbid died—do those two things with anyone else. The times changed, and articles on divorce and extramarital affairs began to appear in the women's magazines. Doris, who believed their words when they had been about how to find, catch, and feed Mr. Right, did not want to believe them now. Which is why she was immune to the sly overtures of Henry Conaway, who walked his beagle past her house each day.

"Good morning Doris Lakeman, and my, you are looking lovely in the fullness of this radiant sun," he would say if she was in the front yard.

Doris would look at him, his tumble of words sounding like French to her. He would come into the yard, touch her on the arm, and she'd draw back, slightly.

"Perhaps you would care to join me on a little stroll?" he'd say, undeterred.

Doris was always firm. "I'm married, Henry Conaway, and I do not go on walks with men."

He always laughed when she said this, and touched her once more on the arm before leaving. "Someday, dear Doris, you will join me. I know you will."

Henry Conaway was the only seductive presence in her life, was the only man who attempted to lead her astray. Why, she wondered, not guessing that there might have been other men more alluring than Henry, would women jeopardize their marriages for such silliness?

But apparently they did. All around her, up and down the street and around the block, marriages failed. Each time the news reached her, Doris was shocked. "I don't want to hear about it," she'd say, the only time she'd close her ears to the neighborhood gossip.

There was only one chink in the invincible armor she wrapped around her marriage, and Doris was very good at not thinking about it. She only considered this point of vulnerability when she herself was feeling vulnerable and emotional. It was another one of the terrible "what if's." What if Emmett doesn't love me as much as I love him? What if another woman held out her hand to him? Would he take it? Doris became very dizzy on the rare occasions this appalling "what if" popped into her unwary mind.

She would have become more than dizzy if she had known that many years ago Emmett had indeed taken, and held tightly, another woman's hand.

Billy rode around town on his bicycle, his head filled with precisely the yearnings and fantasies Doris had spent her life avoiding. He had taken the day off and set his mind to a number of useful and distracting enterprises. It was distraction really, rather than usefulness, he sought. When he awakened that morning, feverish and sweaty after another series of erotic bouts with Nelly (he was no longer sure they were dreams—his bed was always so disheveled; his body had the limpness that came only with sexual encounters), he jumped out of bed and immediately started doing things. He thought if he did things, if he was hyperactive and purposeful, he might actually have an hour or two where his thoughts were free of Nelly.

An hour or two. After doing his laundry, cleaning the kitchen, rewiring an old lamp, and painting the front porch steps, Billy had been granted about two non-Nelly minutes. Those two minutes were taken up by his mother, that other demonic force that possessed him.

The phone jangled, demanding immediate attention. Billy put down his brush and hurried into the house, tracking in gray paint with the heel of his sneaker. His mother's dark powers were already at work. He picked up the phone.

A voice, wheezy with cigarette smoke, said, "So, did you get laid off, or what? Why are you answering the phone this time of day?"

Billy was silent a moment. He looked down the hall at his sneaker tracks, like the footprints of the Invisible Man. "Mom. If you didn't expect me to be here, why did you call?"

There was the sound of a deep inhale on a cigarette. "I call every day." The breath let out.

"You call every day? You call even though I'm not here and you know it?" The woman must have taken courses in torturing offspring. At the graduate level. God. He thought of the phone ringing day after day, month after month, his mother puffing cigarettes on the other end. How long did she let it ring?

"I have nothing to do, so I call."

"Mom, don't say that. You have plenty to do."

There was no reply. Billy heard a match strike. "You smoke too much."

"Smoking's one of the things I do. You want me to do something? I smoke."

Billy's mother was not a happy woman. She had never been a whole lot of fun, but when Billy's father left her in March after thirty-five years of marriage, she emerged from her chrysalis of mere unfun into the insect embodiment of pure seething misery. Billy imagined his mother as an insect, a fat bug sitting at home on the fading sofa with a cigarette dangling from her jagged mandibles. Billy's father just walked out the door that March day. He called Billy from the train station. He said, "Son, your mother's a miserable person and I'm leaving her. I've put in my thirty-five years and that's it." He sounded like a man who had done hard time.

A husband could leave his wife, but unfortunately the mother–son bond was something else. Billy was kind to his mother. He listened to her tired voice on the phone when she called; he went around to her place and fixed things for her; he stopped by to visit. But there was never a moment when he heard her voice or sat near her on the sofa, that he did not remember with sympathy that his father took the afternoon train out of her life.

Billy hung up after a few more minutes of listening to his mother smoke. The reason she called was to invite him for supper. Of course he accepted. Hot diggety—supper with Ma. Those were the two minutes out of the entire morning he spent not thinking of Nelly. Two minutes of sadness, and when the phone hit the receiver, it was back to love.

Sadness and love. The two blended together and made him frantic. He needed physical release, wanted to exhaust himself so that he could flop down in bed and just conk out. No dreams, no thoughts of sadness and love.

So Billy got on his red three-speed bicycle, the one he'd owned since eighth grade, and dashed along the streets of Gramenton. He pedaled like a wild man. He pretended he was in a race, pretended he was being chased by a motorcycle gang. The sweat popped out and blew into his eyes. He squinted and did not see his mailman friends who waved and called to him as he whizzed by. Up and down the streets he went, in and out of neighborhoods, without direction or destination.

But not really. Even in his frenzied state Billy had a growing sense that he wasn't going up and down Gramenton, but round and round in an ever tightening circle. He was speeding along on the edge of a whirlpool, and in the vortex of the swirling water sat the home of Nelly Lakeman. That was the sense he had, of being sucked into a whirlpool. He was heading for Nelly's house, heading for the source, the center of his turmoil. And what, for heaven's sake, was he going to do when he got there? Propose to her? Tear off her clothes, tear off his clothes? Tell her he loved her?

That seemed to be the most logical thing. Billy stopped his bike a moment, but his thoughts continued to race around. Yes, he'd tell her he loved her. Nelly was a wise, sensible woman. No doubt she'd handle his declaration gracefully, offer him guidance and counsel. What he really wanted was to hop in the sack with her, like in the dreams. But that was not going to happen. He wasn't a home wrecker. He wouldn't do that to Max. Not that there was any chance of him coming between Max and Nelly, co-owners of the best marriage in town.

Nelly, he'd say, I've got a problem, a serious problem. I don't know why, I don't know how, but I'm in love with you. I'm not happy about this, believe me, and I know you're not happy to hear it. I probably shouldn't be telling you this, I'm probably wrecking everything, but I don't know what else to do.

Billy started up again, and this time he headed straight for Nelly. He'd tell her and they'd take it from there. It was the best he could do. Everything would be okay, just get it out in the open, he told himself. Then he had a thought. If Nelly opened the door in her nurse's uniform, in the erotic outfit of his dreams, he might do something foolish like touch her. He licked the sweat off his upper lip and continued forward, deciding that was a chance he was just going to have to take.

Mrs. Legland's was the last lawn before Max went next door to Mrs. Zeno. He was very tired, overdoing it for a man the first day back on the job. Most of what he had cut was three weeks' growth, although some of his customers had gathered up the strength to sit behind their rarely used mowers. He wished they hadn't. It pained him to see hastily cut grass, lawns cut in boredom and anger. The chopped spots, places torn by mowers adjusted to the wrong height—the yards were battered bodies, and Max treated them tenderly, spreading fertilizer now that it was fall, raking up the few scattered leaves as if cleansing a wound.

Mrs. Legland sat in her usual place in the sun watching him, or at least pointing her blind face in his direction so she appeared to be watching him.

When Max stopped his mower to rest, she said, "Again? That's the third time you've stopped."

"I've been sick, Mrs. Legland." He'd explained this to her twice already.

"Even so," she said.

Max smiled. The woman was consistent, and in a world that was increasingly inconsistent, she was a comfort of sorts.

"I was thinking of hiring that other boy when you didn't show up."

"Clement Strokas?"

"That's the one." Mrs. Legland turned her cloudy gaze on him.

"You'd have regretted it." Clement and Mrs. Legland deserved each other. He'd have liked to have seen them go a few rounds.

"Well, maybe. At least he wouldn't be sick all the time."

Max let that one pass.

"I almost asked him, too. He showed up here a couple of times. Hayward, my gardener, saw him poking around."

"Poking around?" Max felt a little twinge in his belly, near his incision.

"Hayward said so." Mrs. Legland leered, the gaps in her teeth big enough to stick a finger through. "I thought he might be drumming up business, but Hayward said no. Say, where's your cat?"

Max gestured. "Over there lying in the sun." Bilko lay stretched out on her back like a baby seal, feet dangling like flippers. "Well, what did Hayward say he was doing?"

"Who?" Mrs. Legland damn well knew who. She enjoyed playing forgetful, keeping the agitation level up.

"Clement."

"Oh, him." Mrs. Legland leaned close, her sour breath escaping through her gappy teeth. "Hayward said he was looking at the house next door."

The twinge moved from Max's belly up to his head and down to his groin. Clement spying on the Zeno's. Oh, Christ.

"Looking at the house?" he managed to say.

"From what Hayward tells me, that place is worth a look these days." Mrs. Legland raised her cane and pointed at the Zeno's. Max could see bits of the house through the trees and shrubbery.

"Hayward's seen things."

"Things?"

"One day he saw flashes of light coming from one of the rooms. Another time he said there was an eagle and a dove sitting on chairs on the side porch, and when he blinked, the birds turned into a man and a woman. How about that?"

A dove. An eagle.

"Now of course, that's Hayward talking, and I'm at a serious disadvantage depending on Hayward for the local news. Hayward, as we are all aware, has been known to row his boat with one oar out of the water.

"But," she went on, "I've seen the light flashing at night, too. Could be my glaucoma, could be the Mr. taking dirty pictures of the Mrs."

"Could be," said Max weakly.

Mrs. Legland peered at her bare wrist as if checking the time. "Well, I'm not paying you to bend my ear, am I? Less gossip and more work might keep you from getting sick all the time."

Max left his pickup in front of Mrs. Legland's. He put Bilko on the front seat, and when he did, the dog did something she'd never done before. She clamped down on the cuff of his jacket and would not let go. Max pulled and yanked and finally had to pry her jaws open. Bilko slumped down on the seat and looked away from him.

"Listen," he said. "I'll only be a little while, I promise."

No response.

"Bilko, I'm sorry. I can't help it." He closed the door on her and looked up and down the street. There was no one in sight. He eased past Mrs. Legland, still sitting in her backyard talking to herself, or maybe talking and unable to see that nobody was there. Max ducked through the privet hedge and slipped over the picket fence into Mrs. Zeno's yard. The grass had not grown an inch since he cut it three weeks ago. Mrs. Zeno managed that somehow, no doubt. He would have to explain to her that cutting her lawn was his excuse for being there, that cutting grass was what he *did*. He stopped beside an oak and stared up into its branches, and beyond them to the sky. If there had been an eagle, Max would have been across the yard and back over the fence in two leaps. But he was safe. He slid into the side porch and raised his hand to tap on the door.

The door opened before his knuckles hit the wood. Mrs. Zeno drew him in and lifted him off the floor in an embrace.

"How I missed you, Max!"

She kissed him many times, pulling back to look at his face, then kissing him again.

"And you," she said, "did you miss me?"

"I missed you terribly." It was true. With each kiss he understood how much he had missed her.

She took him by the hand and led him into the white room, pulled him to the pallet and began to undress him. She placed a finger on his belly and traced along his scar.

"So, you have met my husband," she said.

"Yeah, about that—" Max began.

She placed a finger on his lips. It tasted of honey. "He does not know. Believe me, he does not know."

Max believed her; he listened to her voice with its sweet accent and believed her. She sounded like Ingrid Bergman now, the fantasy woman of his teenage years, her words low and lilting. It was a voice you trusted, the voice Cary and Humphrey trusted. Max tried to remember how those movies came out.

"You sound different," he said, kissing her breasts.

"I sound the way you want me to sound," she murmured in her Ingrid accent.

This was a woman who knew how to please. At times, as they made love slowly on the pallet, Max would half open his eyes and see Ingrid's eyes, or lips, a lock of Ingrid's soft brown hair. They did not make love with abandon as they had that first Thursday, but it was still exquisite. When it was over, Max felt as if he had slept with several women at the same time. Certainly, Max knew by now, Mrs. Zeno was capable of such a feat. If she could be Ingrid, she could be anyone. Once, at the end, for the briefest instant, he even thought he saw Nelly, her features blending with Mrs. Zeno's. It was quite a moment.

She sighed, her sweet breath warm on his cheek. She lifted her hand and put each of her fingers to his lips, one by one. The first finger tasted of lemon, the second of cinnamon, the third peppermint, and her baby finger of vanilla. He licked each one.

"You can do anything," Max said after a time.

Mrs. Zeno pulled away from him and laughed, then came close again. "When I am in love, I can do anything."

Max went up on one elbow and stared hard at her. "I think I may be falling in love with you, too," he heard himself say. And then quickly he followed those words with, "But I'm married."

"Yes, Max, I am married also."

"Well, I love my wife." He was not so far gone that he did not know that. "How about you?"

"With me it is different." Mrs. Zeno got up and walked

over to one of the white columns in the corner of the room. She made no sound as she moved, as if she was a being without weight or substance. "My husband and I have a very complicated relationship."

"I'll bet." Max began to dress.

She watched him, looking very sad. Those Ingrid eyes, at the misty airfield in Casablanca. "You are leaving me."

Don't speak, Max thought. If you keep talking, I won't be able to go. "I have to."

"What if," she said. "What if I asked you to stay?"

Max walked across the marble floor to her. He put his hand gently on her mouth. "Please don't. I'm married, I have children. Please don't ask me."

Clement, perched in a tree outside the house, saw only a few seconds of Max and Mrs. Zeno together on the pallet before the thin branch gave way beneath him. He fell five feet and landed in the pachysandra, unharmed.

He leaned against the tree laughing to himself. Oh, what a lovely fucking sight, Max Lakeman getting a wiggle on. If only he'd brought a camera. What a snapshot that would have made. Didn't matter, though. The deed was done, done and witnessed by Clement C. Strokas.

Clement had trailed Max all morning. It was pathetically easy. All he had to do was park his truck around the corner and dodge behind a few trees. When Max finished old bitch Legland's place, he began acting sneaky, looking all around, and Clement knew he was about to do something. So he cut into the Zeno's when Max disappeared inside, and climbed the tree.

The tree of knowledge. Clement laughed at his little joke. He didn't know shit about the Bible except that part. That's pretty good, he thought. I climbed the ol' tree of knowledge and saw Adam Lakeman and Eve Zeno going at it like monkeys. He was sorry the limb broke—it was a pretty good show.

You never can tell what you might learn when you climb the right tree.

Well, it was time to share his knowledge. Clement crouched and ran across the yard, keeping to the shadows, then hopped over the fence. Back at his truck he smoked a cigarette, feeling slightly uneasy. Then he said, as if finishing out loud a conversation he'd been having in his head, "Tough shit for him," and started up his truck.

And so Clement Strokas set out on the streets of Gramenton, heading for the same place at the same time as Billy Dalton. Clement got there first. He pulled in front of Max's and Nelly's and stared out his window at the place. It was as neat and tidy as Max's life, or rather as that life used to be. Clement's intention was to scuff things up a little, take some of the shine off. Max had it coming, he was ripe for the fall.

There was a car in the driveway. Clement stubbed a cigarette out on the front walk, wiped his greasy hands on his pants, and rang the doorbell. He looked around for that goddamn dog of theirs, then remembered Max always had it with him. He relaxed, then tensed up again when Nelly answered the door.

Clement's first thought was, She's pretty, and when she smiled, he almost felt bad. Then it pissed him off to think Max got the pretty ones, especially when he remembered his own skinny wife waiting at home for him. Waiting for him? No, just waiting.

"Clement, what a surprise."

Clement took his cap off, then felt stupid, like he was a servant or a nigger or something, and pushed his cap back on his head.

"Yeah, well, I guess it is." A big surprise. He wet his lips with his tongue.

Nelly watched his tongue, quick and darting, and thought of a lizard. What is this lizard doing on my front porch? she wondered. She had never been as charitable as Max in her regard for Clement.

"You want to come in?" She hoped he didn't. She had just vacuumed and didn't want bits of Clement sloughing off on her rug, his dirt, his dead lizard scales.

"I have some news for you, Nelly."

Nelly's first thought, as is true with all nurses and specialists in human disaster, was that something had happened to Max. Since it was Clement telling her, it probably involved a lawn mower, Max's hand. Max had been doing him a favor, fixing one of Clement's mowers.

"What hospital?" Nelly said, tightening her grip on the door so that the scalpel cut on her hand stretched. She flinched.

"Hospital?" Then he got it. "Oh, no, no. Not that. He ain't dead or nothing."

Nelly felt a little weak, then foolish. "You scared me, Clement."

"I didn't mean to." Christ, if he didn't say it now, he wouldn't at all.

"Then what news?" she said, tilting her head slightly.

Here we go, he thought. "I figured you might want to know that Max is sleeping with a lady up on Guernsey Road."

Nelly stared at him, her mouth coming slightly open. She moved forward and Clement edged back.

"Clement," she said, her voice tight, "you're a sack of shit."

"Maybe so. But I climbed a tree and saw them. She lives on Guernsey Road. Max, he'll tell you."

"You climbed a tree? You climbed a tree to spy on my husband?"

"Yeah. I climbed a fucking tree, how about that?" He started down the steps, keeping his eye on her so she didn't jump on his back or do something crazy.

"You feel good now, Clement? You feel pretty good?" Her voice was getting loud.

"Yeah, I guess I do. How about yourself?" He turned and walked back to his truck, an exaggerated swagger to his step. He got in and took a last look at Nelly, standing still in the open doorway. He gunned the engine, took off, and almost ran over Billy pedaling around the corner on his bicycle. Clement gave him the finger as he drove by.

Billy had come to tell Nelly he loved her. He was going to do it, he was going to do it. He pedaled up the driveway, and there she was waiting in the doorway for him. Was she waiting for him? Billy dropped his bicycle on the grass and ran up the sidewalk to her. He rushed up the front porch steps and was just about to speak, to tell her, when she made an indescribable little noise and fell into his arms.

Clement, meanwhile, drove over to Boothwyn, two towns over from Gramenton, to see his folks and do their lawn for them. His father had emphysema and couldn't push a mower more than four steps without turning blue. Clement, for the most part, liked his parents, or at least didn't have anything particular against them.

All the way to Boothwyn he felt kind of neutral. Telling Nelly was not the kick he had imagined it would be. Well, it didn't matter. The point was to stick a bug up Max's ass anyway.

He went in to the kitchen where his mother stood over a table rolling out dough. She was a heavy woman with graying red hair. There was a smudge of flour on her cheek.

"Hey, Mom, how's it going?" He kissed her forehead. "Where's Dad?"

"Down at the shop. He should be home soon."

Clement sat down at the other end of the table.

"What's new?" he said.

"Same old thing. Your father does too much. I complain.

You know how it goes." She pressed her fingers into the dough. "And you? What's the good word from Gramenton?"

And for some reason, probably because it was the only thing on his mind, and because he didn't feel too pleased with himself about it, Clement told his mother about going to Nelly. She listened quietly, embarrassed for him. He was not a happy man; he did stupid things, did not know when to speak and when not to. She was about to shush him up when he said a name. A piece of dough slipped from her hands in a lump on to the table.

"You said Lakeman?" she whispered.

"Yeah." He looked at her. "Max's last name is Lakeman. Why?"

His mother sat down. "And Max," she said, the words barely coming out, "he has a father?"

"Mom, what's wrong? Sure, he has a father. Emmett or Emory Lakeman, I think. He used to be a conductor or something."

"Oh, Clement," she said. Her eyes went blurry.

"What did I do?" Clement's stomach did a nervous turn.

"Max. Did he do something to you, that you told on him?"

"He's a schmuck. He cheated on his wife, so I told her. What's wrong with that?"

"Did he do something to you?"

"I don't know—he cheated, Mom. What difference does it make?" Clement picked off a piece of dough and rolled it over and over. It turned brown, then black from the engine grease on his fingers.

His mother reached for his hand. "Am I a bad person?"

"No." What was she doing?

"Clement, listen to me. Just listen." She started to cry and then caught herself. "You're right. I'm not a bad person. But once, very long ago, I was with a man, and this man was cheating on his wife. And because I knew this, I was cheating, too. He was a good man, and there was no reason for his wife to know, no reason for someone like you to tell her."

This was not a story Clement wanted to hear. He stood up. He went over to the window and looked out, rolled the black ball of dough between his fingers.

His mother told him the story he didn't want to hear.

· 9 ·

STUNNED, Billy stood on the front porch with Nelly in his arms. She was in his arms, he could smell her hair, he could see the soft down on the back of her neck.

Had Nelly been having the dreams, too? Billy wondered what form they took, how graphic their erotic content. Nelly was always dressed (for the few moments she *was* dressed) in her nurse's uniform, all white with plenty of pink flesh. How was he dressed in her dreams, as a mailman? The mailman and the nurse, by day an ordinary working couple. By night . . .

Billy felt her shiver, then she made a kind of wet, throaty noise.

"I know, I know," he said softly.

Nelly pulled away and stared at him. There were tears on her cheeks, her nose was running. "You know?"

Billy stared back at her, suddenly very confused. Tears of joy? No, he didn't think your nose ran like that when you were joyful. In fact, with her red face and frantic eyes, Nelly looked anything but. Billy didn't know what to say. She had been in his arms, and now this.

Nelly's face went through several more changes, all of them sad and wondering. "You said you know, Billy. Is that true? Come on, talk to me."

This was definitely not the time to confess his love. She was expecting something from him, but what he had no idea.

"Nelly, I—I don't know anything," he stammered. "You were crying, so I . . ."

She was in his arms again, her tears accompanied now by low, mournful sounds. Billy held her for a time, then guided her gently inside the house. He had never seen her cry before. He sat with his hand on her shoulder, immersed in sadness and love.

After a time Nelly said, her voice quiet and strained, "I don't even know why I'm crying."

Billy didn't move a muscle.

"I mean," she went on, pushing her fingers through her hair, "Clement Strokas is such a . . ."

Billy spoke. "Clement?" He remembered Clement swerving away in his truck, giving him the finger. "He did something?"

"Said something." Nelly's voice broke. Then she got quiet and her eyes narrowed. "Why am I believing him? Why am I sitting here getting so upset?"

She turned and looked at Billy, an angry smile on her face. "Why?"

"What did he say?" It made Billy sick to even think of Clement near Nelly. He had known Clement since his high school days. He was ratty and mean then, and age had not improved him. Clement's specialty was torment—tormenting his poor skinny wife, tormenting his customers, his worn-out lawn mowers. Now Nelly.

"Billy, could you get me a glass of water, do you think?" Nelly said.

She was standing by the window when Billy returned. Without turning around she said, in a voice so soft and far away Billy had to close his eyes to hear it, to make sense of it, "Max is sleeping with someone." Then she suddenly whirled and faced him. "Clement said Max is sleeping with some woman over on Guernsey Road."

Without thinking, Billy began drinking from the glass of water. He drank all of it, then looked down at the bottom of the glass and spoke into it, the sound of his voice empty and echoing. "Clement's a liar."

"I believe him, Billy. I don't know why, but I do." She walked past Billy to the sofa. She sat down. She got up and paced. She sat down again.

"I know what he is, but why would he bother to make this up? I don't even think he's smart enough to make it up. He was like a little boy who found out something dirty, and he just couldn't wait to poke in it. He's never liked Max, he's jealous of him, and he found his big chance to get back at him. He said he climbed a tree, Billy. He climbed a goddamn tree to spy on Max. Anybody who'd admit to that could not be lying."

"But Max loves you." Billy's voice was high and upset.

"Oh, Billy." Nelly went over to him and placed a hand on his cheek, offering him comfort now. "I know he loves me. But that doesn't always protect you."

"You guys have the perfect marriage. Max wouldn't. Clement's lying."

"Maybe, Billy. Maybe he is, but I don't think so. Max has been weird lately. I mean, I know he gets weird, but he's been different. Distant, distracted. Something."

Billy had not noticed. Whenever he was with Max these days, he himself was so distracted he saw nothing. Max could have sprouted elephant ears and an extra leg, and Billy would not have been aware of the change. Now he felt guilty. Had there been warning signs, could he have talked to Max? Then he had a thought.

"He's been sick. Maybe that threw him off. You know how crazy and sensitive he is."

Nelly was silent a moment. "I don't think so, Billy. He's been strange for a while now. If Clement hadn't said something, I might not have seen it. But the last month or two, thinking about it, he's been different. He has."

"Jeez," said Billy. "We're not even giving him a chance. One word from Clement, and *pow*."

Nelly looked at him. "He'll get his chance as soon as he gets home." Her voice broke and she started to cry again. "We do have a perfect marriage. Max could sleep with a thousand women and it wouldn't matter. It doesn't matter. He loves me. I just wish, I just wish . . ."

What she wished for was a miracle. Maybe she would look up and see the hands on the kitchen clock turn backward—her meeting with Clement would have never occurred; she would never know Max had cheated on her. But the hands moved steadily forward, without pity. She knew and would always know. This is what I get for looking at Dr. Zeno, she thought. This is what I get for enjoying one brief moment in another man's arms. But I did not linger there, I did not linger there.

Billy stayed with her for a time, this woman of his dreams. He did not, of course, tell her what he had come to say. When she quieted down again, he left her sitting on the sofa with her runny nose. He turned once to look at her and was stricken with her beauty, runny nose and all. He got back on his red, three-speed bike and pedaled frantically up and down the darkening streets of Gramenton until he thought his heart would burst.

Doris and Emmett were walking around their yard after supper.

Emmett bent over and picked some leaves off the marigolds.

"You know," he said, "everything goes so fast. Wasn't spring just here a minute ago? And now look. Leaves are coming down all over everything, it's getting cold." He sighed and shook his head.

"The seasons change, dear," Doris said.

He looked at her. "I know that. That's not what I mean. I'm talking about time, time going too damn fast."

Emmett the conductor and Time. The older he got, the more he felt as though he was on a speeding train that was coming into all the stations ahead of schedule. He was looking out of the windows and everything was a blur. Before he knew it, he'd be at the last stop and the long train ride would be over.

"Listen," Doris said suddenly, craning her neck. "Geese. Do you hear them?" She pointed. "Look!"

Emmett looked, moving his head slowly. He had a touch of arthritis in his neck. There they were, going south, *zoom, zoom, zoom*. Before you knew it they'd be heading north again. Ticktock, back and forth, another mark of the passage of time.

Doris took his hand, gently at first, then so hard he winced.

"Emmett, do you love me?" Seeing the geese reminded her of her fall honeymoon with Emmett, thirty-five years ago. The geese always did that, pulled her thoughts to the time on the blanket, when they had lain together watching the clouds, and the geese, their tremendous open triangle stretching across the sky, seemed an omen of love and hope. Back then, Doris saw such signs everywhere. But the geese stayed with her, a little touch of possibility reborn for brief moments each fall.

Her question caught Emmett off guard. He tried to get his hand back, but she wouldn't let go.

"Do you love me?" she said again.

"Yes." He kissed her forehead, her cheek. When she pouted her lips, he kissed them, too. She released him, and his hand throbbed slightly.

"Do you love me as much as you used to?" She was having one of her emotional moments.

"More," said Emmett. He spoke the truth. He did love her. More, less, was not the way he really thought of it; he simply loved her.

Doris stopped and looked away from him, picking at a leaf that had dropped onto her sleeve. She asked him a question she had never asked before, had never wanted to ask. It dropped into her mind, suddenly, like the leaf she now plucked at apprehensively.

"Emmett, have there ever been any other women?"

Emmett walked on a little ahead of her and slid both his hands into his pockets where they trembled slightly against his legs. All this time and now Doris pops the question. How would he have answered her years and years ago when he'd walk into the apartment, go back home to her, after an evening in bed with Miriam Rodolfo? What if she'd been in the doorway then, what if she had asked him? Would he have told her about Miriam?

Emmett paused and listened to the last of the geese, honking in the distance, the sad sound dying in the chill air. Then he turned and put his arms around Doris and told her, said the same words he would have if she had asked him a long time ago.

"No. Never. There has never been anyone but you."

They stood together for a while, holding on, both of them trembling in the cold.

Nelly watched Max. She watched him pull into the driveway and get out of the pickup with Bilko. She watched as he walked in the door and kissed her, a kissless kiss, she far away as their lips met. She watched him through dinner, watched the four of them together.

Dinner was a killer. Each time Max smiled at Nora, or did something as ordinary as pass the beans to Ben, Nelly's heart stopped, too full of love and dread to function. Max jeopardized all this for a woman on Guernsey Road? Nelly tried to think of the women she knew on Guernsey Road, and only Mrs. Legland came to mind.

"We drew pumpkins at school today," Ben said to Max. Nelly bit her lip. Too much, too much.

"You did?"

Nelly could see from Max's clouded gaze that the coming

of Halloween was news to him. A distracted man does not notice the change of seasons.

"Yeah," said Ben. "Mine was orange with a black mouth," he said. "First, I did a blue one and Joey said it looked dumb, but Mrs. Raynor said blue was pretty and wanted to hang it up, but then I didn't like blue after all, so I did an orange one, and that one looked okay, so Mrs. Raynor hanged that one up instead, and I threw the blue one out."

Max looked at his son and nodded gravely. "Well, there's a moral in there somewhere," he said. Then he smiled.

"What's a moral?" Ben immediately asked.

"A moral," said Nelly, coming back into the dining room from the kitchen, where she was getting the ice cream, "has to do with telling the difference between right and wrong." She spoke so emphatically her entire family went silent and looked at her.

"A moral," she said again, her voice low, "has to do with the way a person conducts himself."

"Oh," said Ben, with no comprehension whatsoever.

"Here, let me help you with the ice cream," Max said softly, taking the bowls from her and setting up the children.

Everyone ate their ice cream quietly. Bilko sat in the corner of the room without moving, ignoring the piece of meat Max had saved and held out for her under the table.

Nelly waited until the children were put to bed, then held on for another half hour until she was sure they were asleep. Then without a word, she took Max by the hand, led him into the living room, and pulled him to the sofa.

"Hey," Max started.

"No, listen," she said. "I have to make sure of something." She squeezed his hand hard, locked her fingers in his. "You love me, don't you?"

Max stared at the hands clinched together between them. "Nelly, I love you."

"Look at me."

"I love you," he said again. He glanced, for a moment, past her and out the darkened window. He thought he saw a single white feather suspended in the air.

"Clement was by. . . ."

Clement. Ah, Clement. If it came from anyone, it would have to have been Clement. It was almost a natural act, in keeping with the true order of things, coming from Clement.

"And he told you," Max said quietly.

Nelly had had this tiny, tiny hope that he would not know what she was talking about, that he would deny it. Against all her nursing experience, which warned that no one, ever, is spared bad news, she had hoped.

"Why, Max? It's not something you ever wanted to do, I know it." Her eyes were so full of sadness he closed his own against them.

"You're right, it's something I didn't want to do," he whispered. "Until I did it."

"Oh, Max, Max. Don't you remember what you once told me? We were talking about this exact thing. You said that it doesn't make sense to cheat if you're basically happy with whoever you're with. You said that people cheat because they get all confused and they want that thrill again, that kick of holding on to a new body."

She took his face in her hands. "Remember, remember? But then that wears off, it always wears off, and you wind up with somebody who's not much different than the person you cheated on. So why not just stick with the first one, who you love anyway, and spare everybody the turmoil, all the pain?" She took a breath. "Max, everybody's tempted. We're all tempted. You know, I mean, I've looked at other men too, not very often, but I have. The thing is I've never slept with any of them. You look, but Jesus, you don't sleep with them."

Max felt Nelly's hands on his face, the hands that had touched him a thousand times. Yes, he knew all that. And when his world had been ordinary, Nelly's words made sense, for an ordinary lover they made sense. But his lover wasn't

ordinary. She had appeared in a diaphanous robe in the rhododendrons; she had risen naked from the sea; she had led
him to the pallet in the white room.

"Nelly, I don't know how to explain it."

"I'm not asking you to explain it."

"Well, then?"

"Well, then? Max, what do you think I'm asking? Go
upstairs and look at your children. Look at me, this house,
Bilko lying over there on the rug. Max, I'm asking you to stop
it. Jesus Christ, is it worth it?"

Max was silent. His mind went blank. His thoughts were,
for a moment, the color green, the color of grass. He imagined
himself behind a lawn mower on a summer day, pushing his
perfect mower over a perfect lawn. There was no one else
around, not Nelly, not the other woman in white. He was
alone pushing a mower on and on, in a sea of green, and he
was very happy.

When he did not instantly agree with her that it wasn't
worth it, Nelly let go of him and stared at her knees.

"I'm sorry, Nelly, I'm a little lost." He shrugged and she
shrugged back at him.

"What are you going to do?" she asked, her voice very
small.

"I have to do something?" Max said. "You mean like
drastic?"

"Don't leave me," she whispered, and dropped her head
on his shoulder.

"I'm not leaving. What are you saying? Why are we talking like this?"

"We're talking like this because you're sleeping with another woman, and you haven't said any of the things you're
supposed to say, like 'I'll never do it again' or 'I'm sorry, I
must have been out of my mind, will you forgive me?' "

"I am sorry, Nelly."

Her eyes sharpened. "Sorry I found out, or sorry you
did it?"

Max sighed and ran his fingers through his hair. "I'm just sorry."

"Who the hell is this woman on Guernsey Road, anyway? Do I know her?"

"No. You know her husband, though. He did my surgery. Remember? Dr. Zeno."

"You slept," her voice slow and jittery, "with Dr. Zeno's wife?"

"Yes, Mrs. Zeno," Max said. He turned and looked out the window and saw flashes of lightning in the distance. He had not heard thunder, though, and there was no rain. Just great silent slices of lightning. When he turned back, Nelly was over by the hall closet pulling on a jacket.

"What are you doing? Where are you going?"

"Stay here with the children," she said. "Where are the car keys? Oh, here they are." She got them off the mantelpiece, where they sat between a picture of Max and Nelly on their wedding day and one of Ben and Nora playing in the grass with Bilko.

"I'm going to the hospital to find Dr. Zeno."

"Come on, Nelly," Max said, holding on to her arm.

She twisted and pulled him off. "He's always there. He's there even though he should be home with his wife, where all married men belong."

"Nelly, come on, don't bring him into this. There's no point."

She opened the front door and stood there. "You bet I'm going to bring him into this. I'll bring in whoever I have to. And you're wrong, there is a point. The point is to get you back, Max, because I love you. And you love me."

They stood staring at each other until Nelly at last turned and ran out into the night, her figure illuminated by the distant lightning.

There were all sorts of people outside in this strange, silent storm. Clement was sitting on his back steps looking at the sky. The agitated bolts of electricity above him were a large-scale display of the same process going on inside his brain. His thoughts were flashing around, striking here, striking there. Max Lakeman was his half-brother. He hated Max Lakeman. Which meant he hated his own brother, his only brother.

Clement had simply walked out of his mother's house when she told him. He walked right past his truck, didn't even see it, and kept on going the five miles to Gramenton. At one point he stopped and looked in a store window, and instead of himself, he saw the reflection of Max staring back at him. Max in the dirty work clothes of Clement, a scowl on an unshaven face. That is how Clement saw himself, as the distorted reflection of Max. Max was happy, he loved his work, his clean mowers, the lawns. Max had this great family, while Clement's own wife was skinny and miserable, his children unpleasant, his hours behind his run-down mowers infuriating.

Why should he hate Max? He just did, always had. Max is my brother, my *brother*, he thought. Clement's brain flashed all over the place. His mother had said, "You had no reason to hurt Max Lakeman. He's your brother."

"Shit," said Clement. There was a feeling churning in his belly and beginning to creep all through him. It was a feeling that he had experienced very, very rarely in his thirty-two years. It was called remorse, and he hugged himself tightly trying to contain it.

Mrs. Legland was outside, too. The lightning had awakened her. She had fallen asleep in her easy chair while listening to the radio. She opened her eyes at the moment a bolt of lightning lit the sky, and her first thought, pulled as she was from her dreams, was that she could see again.

"Holy cow!" she said, and leapt up and hurried (leaping and hurrying as much as her ancient body would allow) over to the French doors and out into the yard. She wanted to see her flowers. Unfortunately, still being blind and not knowing it, she turned left when she should have turned right, and ended up in the front yard instead of the back, where the garden was.

She also didn't see the large maple root near the sidewalk and caught her slippered right foot on it and landed, after a half somersault, on her back.

A man on his way to the 7-Eleven for a quart of milk and a box of doughnuts saw the whole thing. He stopped his car and ran over to the tiny still figure lying in a flannel nightie in the grass.

He stared at her, quite flustered, wondering if he should administer one of the two lifesaving techniques he'd learned at the YMCA—the Heimlich maneuver or CPR. The woman did not look as if she were choking or suffering a heart attack. She looked out and out dead.

Which is why he jumped two feet into the air when Mrs. Legland suddenly opened her eyes.

"Is that you, Max?"

"Excuse me, ma'am?" he said, when he regained some of his composure.

She glared at him with her dim eyes. "I'm not paying you to just stand around, damn it, Max. Now give me a hand."

The man gave her a hand up; then she shook him off and made her slow way back into her house, muttering furiously.

Billy sat in his lawn chair in his backyard watching the lightning and half hoping that a bolt would come searing down on him and put him out of his misery. Then he thought better of it and hopped up and moved his chair out of the open and onto the patio under the awning. Fried to a crisp was not the way he really wanted to go.

He thought about geometry—straight lines, triangles, and rectangles. The straight line between two perfect points was Max and Nelly before all the trouble started. Nothing purer, simpler, than a straight line. In tenth-grade geometry, as in life, the straight line was the only figure that made sense to him. He remembered doing proofs in that hideous geometry class, and as soon as they came to triangles, the isosceles, the equilateral, the scalene triangle, he began to flounder. The others had no trouble connecting up the A with the B, the B with the C, C back to A. It was no wonder there was no connecting the triangle of Max, Nelly, and Billy. What a lopsided figure it would make—the two great lines of Max and Nelly, the tiny, thin bottom of the triangle that was Billy.

And now the rectangle, what with Max's lover on Guernsey Road thrown in. The rectangle, with its sickening permutations the trapezoid and the rhombus, was the most impossible of all. The tears caused by rectangles, he remembered them well. He broke his math teacher's patience with his inability to grasp the ever-changing proportions of that quadrangular nightmare.

Really, though, he was no part of those figures. Since he had never told Nelly he loved her, he was the invisible one, filling out the lines only in his mind. The rectangle had three solid sides, and his side was the sketchy theoretical one that his math teacher would have drawn as a dotted line.

Billy loved a woman who loved a man who loved, or at least slept with, another woman. Even viewed in that barebones way the situation was impossible. His thoughts moved to another kind of math, from geometry to probability. Watching the flickering lightning, he wondered which he had more chance of, being struck by lightning or striking up a love affair with Nelly?

He felt ratty even having such thoughts. He should be rallying to his friends' sides, helping in some way to mend their marriage, offering counsel. Why had Max done such a thing? What sort of woman could have possibly lured him from Nelly? Or was Max the one who did the luring, as unlikely as that seemed?

Billy decided on the noblest course of action. He would be there for both of his friends, in whatever way they needed him. He sighed. Oh well, it was sacrificial, and therefore honorable. And then another bit of rattiness crept in again—

if, after all his noble attempts, their marriage still failed, what was the socially correct mourning period before he could begin courting Nelly?

Miriam Rodolfo Strokas and Emmett Lakeman, lying miles apart in their separate beds, were both watching the flashing lightning and thinking of each other. They were remembering, as they always did when the sky flashed, the time they were together in Miriam's apartment making love and a sudden thunderstorm knocked out the city's electricity. Miriam got up and lit a candle, and then they lay in her bed next to the window, looking out into the pure dark. Soon other candles in other rooms began to appear, little dots of flickering gold. Emmett and Miriam pretended that each candle lit meant that another couple had made love. The city of Boothwyn, all aflame, was a grand confirmation of their secret coupling. They lit another candle and went at it again.

Now, in bed once more, each with an old and familiar partner, there was no lovemaking on this night filled with great silent streaks of light. Now no one got out of bed to find a candle. Emmett frowned slightly and stared up at the dark ceiling. And several miles away, Miriam placed a tentative hand on her sleeping husband's shoulder, then slowly pulled it back again.

Nelly parked her car in the employees' lot behind Forkton Community Hospital. Down in the doctors' section she saw the purple convertible, the color of passion, owned by Dr. and Mrs. Zeno.

Nick Simmons, the hospital security guard, hurried across the lot to her.

"Hey, Nelly, how about this lightning, huh? I mean, Jesus, you ever see anything like it?" He was shouting, as if he was trying to be heard above a storm, but there was no noise.

"Sure is something, Nick. You be careful out here." She looked up. The lightning was high above them, most of it directly over the hospital grounds. None of the bolts were striking anywhere, though. They hovered in the air in an agitated way, like churning bees that had not yet found a focus for their wrath.

Nelly went straight to a phone in the hospital lobby and dialed Dr. Zeno's beeper number, then hung up and waited. She picked up the phone again on the first ring. It was an ICU nurse answering for Dr. Zeno.

"I'm sorry, Dr. Zeno is in a code," she said.

Nelly recognized the voice. "Janice, this is Nelly. Who's coding?"

"Oh, hi, Nelly. Bed 6, Mr. Haines. He's been going bad all night. Dr. Zeno's not having much luck—they've been working on him for half an hour. I think Zeno's about to call the code."

"Well, I'm coming down. See you in a few minutes."

When she got there, the code was indeed over. All the nurses, doctors, respiratory technicians, and other team members who had crammed into the room were filing out of it now. In the center of the little room, dead in his bed and laced with IV tubes, respirator tubes, and electrode wires, was Mr. Haines. It was not a peaceful scene.

She watched as Dr. Zeno, looking grim, conferred briefly with two other doctors, then started out of the unit. She grabbed his arm as he went by. He turned, looked hard at her for a moment, then they walked out together and across the hall to a waiting area. Nelly let go of him and he continued walking, pacing back and forth, his huge white-suited figure filling the space around him.

"So, it's you," he said in his thick accent. His voice was tired. He reached in his coat pocket, pulled out a crumpled pack of cigarettes and lit one.

"You smoke?" said Nelly. She was very surprised. It didn't fit. Then, thinking of something else that didn't fit, she said, "Mr. Haines died."

Dr. Zeno stopped pacing for a moment and exhaled smoke

as he answered. "Yes and yes, dear Nelly. Which surprises you more?" He half smiled, then started to move again.

"I've never seen one of your patients die before."

"And you thought I was the miracle worker, infallible, yes?"

"Yes."

"So now you know. All is not what it seems. The world is full of surprises, and that is what makes life interesting." He stopped and looked down at her, one of his eyebrows raised. "And so I find it interesting, but somehow not surprising, that you have sought me out tonight."

"You know why I'm here," said Nelly in a low voice.

Dr. Zeno laughed. "Nelly, Nelly. You have already forgotten. I smoke cigarettes, and poor Mr. Haines has died this night. I'm not infallible, nor am I omniscient."

"Your wife," Nelly started slowly, then hesitated. Dr. Zeno's face instantly darkened. Nelly looked past him and saw through the window a streak of lightning touch down on the hospital's front lawn.

"My . . . wife," he said.

In the distance, for the first time, there was thunder. The wind picked up, blowing dry leaves off the trees.

When she stared at his eyes, she saw anger—the anger of husbands and wives, wives and husbands—and something else, too, something pushing in at the edges. Sadness. Anger and sadness, husbands and wives, were things she also knew.

"Tell me about my wife," said Dr. Zeno.

Nelly hesitated. She thought of Clement bringing the news to her. Everybody telling on everybody.

"Come now, I must know." He touched her arm and she flinched. He pulled back and raised his hands in the air in protest. "I am not going to hurt you."

"I know. I know that." She didn't want this man to touch her. Only Max will touch me, she thought.

"But you must tell me about my wife."

"I find it very hard to believe you don't know. I mean, you were certainly up to something with me."

"Up to something?"

"Jesus, Dr. Zeno," Nelly blurted out. "Up to something. Like Max and your wife."

"Yes?"

She looked at him and saw that he still didn't understand. "Your wife," she said slowly, as if she was translating an impossibly difficult language, "is sleeping with my husband."

A great crash of thunder shook the hospital and forks of lightning lit the sky. Nelly pushed back against the wall.

"I'm sorry, I'm sorry. I do not mean to do that. It is just something that happens." Even as he spoke, the sky became calmer, the thunder receding.

Dr. Zeno lowered his great body into a chair and was silent for a time. He lit another cigarette and stared down at the floor.

At last, he spoke again. "Ah well, I knew it was something, of course. But the details escaped me."

Nelly walked over to him. Even sitting, he was almost as tall as she was. "I want Max back. I'm telling you—I don't want you fooling with me the way you've been, and I want you to stop your wife from fooling with Max."

Dr. Zeno smiled. "Nelly, it is not a matter of stopping my wife. Quite the opposite. You must stop your husband."

Nelly's mouth opened slightly, and she tilted her head, unable to reply.

Dr. Zeno pulled a chair over and motioned for her to sit. "Listen to me. Perhaps you will understand, perhaps not. You have often asked me who I am." He looked at her through a veil of cigarette smoke. "I am here, my wife is here, because of Max. A little has to do with you, but mostly it is Max. Let me ask you. Max, he is a strange man in some way?"

"I love him," said Nelly, unsure.

"That is not what I asked. Max is different, yes? He is

someone who sees things, who has a great imagination? He is someone, I am sure, who has not closed himself to possibilities."

Nelly shut her eyes and tried to envision Max's world. It was a world, she was certain, that was entirely open to possibilities.

Dr. Zeno went on. "I would venture to say that Max is a man who has always known, to put it as he might, that something is out there. Dear Nelly"—he exhaled a great cloud of smoke—"Mrs. Zeno and I are part of what is out there."

"You're not real, then?" She wished Max was here. This was his territory.

"Which real?" said Dr. Zeno. "To Max, we are real. And to you . . . we are real to you, too, because of Max."

"Because of Max?"

"In the best marriages, Nelly, in marriages like yours, when one of you begins to speak, the other is often able to finish the sentence. You are *known* to each other. And sometimes it goes further, sometimes what one of you sees, the other sees, too. Max has seen us, Nelly. And what he sees, to a certain extent, so do you."

Dr. Zeno ran a big hand through his gray curls, then went on. "But Max, it seems, has gone too far. He has slept with Mrs. Zeno. You and I . . . you were always safe, Nelly. You were always safe, so I played, and so did you, a little. But Max, sleeping with my wife . . . Max's imagination is taking him too far."

"You mean"—Nelly's face was flushed—"Max has brought your wife, imagined her, whatever you call it, so he can sleep with her?"

"That is only part of it. But you are thinking in purely physical terms, which is to be expected. You would be lucky if that is all it was. Listen very carefully. You, Nelly, have an imagination, too. *But not like Max.*"

"But not like Max," Nelly repeated, her voice a whisper.

"You know the boundaries of reality. Max does not. When

Max sleeps with my wife, when he puts his arms around her, he is embracing his imagination. He is giving up the real that he has shared with you, for a reality he has imagined into being. I am afraid Max is in danger of choosing a world elsewhere, a world he has half lived in all of his life. You must hope he is merely infatuated with my wife, but not in love with the other reality that she is."

Nelly made a sound, a cry, and jumped up. "You've got to stop her!"

"Nelly, Nelly, it's Max who must be stopped, who must stop himself."

"No."

"Yes. I can do nothing."

She stepped back from him, began to move. "I'm not going to let this happen. He's my husband. I love him. The children."

"I don't know what you can do," said Dr. Zeno. "It depends on Max, how far—"

Nelly started for the door. "I'll put my arms around him. Embrace him, hold him. He doesn't want your wife, and I don't want you. I just . . . I just have to get my arms around him." And she was gone, her feet slapping against the linoleum as she ran.

Dr. Zeno sat in the dark for a long time, smoking cigarettes.

· 10 ·

*M*AX stood on the porch steps staring out into his dark backyard. When the lightning flashed, he saw the outline of the rhododendrons. When the lightning flashed again, he saw her standing there.

This time she was not dressed in a white diaphanous robe. She was wearing pants and a light jacket. Over her shoulder hung a purse, and in her right hand she held a suitcase. Mrs. Zeno was going somewhere.

She was leaving him and she had come to say good-bye. Max stood motionless as she approached, swallowing back his sadness. He looked at the lawn as she walked toward him, and when it was lit by the lightning, the grass seemed black. When she left, she would take the green of the grass, the smell of his mowers, the heat and light of his summer days with her.

Mrs. Zeno reached the porch steps. "Max," she said, her voice breathless and urgent. "He knows."

Max didn't understand, his ears ready for different words. "He knows?"

"My husband, my husband! He knows about us."

Max looked at her suitcase, then back up to her face.

"The lightning," she said. "I know what it means. He must have found out."

Max fell back against the side of the house, and Mrs.

Zeno dropped her suitcase and ran up the steps to him. They wrapped their arms around each other.

"Oh, Jesus," he whispered in her hair. Then, "Does this mean you're leaving? Your suitcase . . . ?"

She pulled back and, for the first time, smiled. "My sweet, sweet Max. I have not come to say good-bye."

Max closed his eyes and for a moment smiled, too, hugged her more tightly.

"No," she went on. "Not good-bye. But I am leaving. And I want you to come with me."

His eyes opened. "What?"

"You must, Max. My husband knows. We cannot stay here."

"I can't leave."

"If you want to be with me, you must leave."

"But I'm happy here, too," he said, his voice shaking.

"Max." She touched his face. "You cannot have everything."

"But I thought we would just spend some time together."

"You know yourself it has gone beyond that. 'Some time together' is not enough time."

"I don't know." He pulled away from her and turned toward his house, looked inside the kitchen door. Bilko was sitting on the kitchen floor, perfectly still, watching the two of them.

"Come with me, Max."

"I can't. I can't leave my children. Leave Nelly."

"They will be safe, I promise you. Your wife will be home soon, I know this."

"Well, I should talk to her at least."

"There is nothing to say that has not been said."

"Maybe . . . maybe I could go with you for just a little while, do you think? Just to see."

"For a little while, then. Yes, Max, but we must go now." Mrs. Zeno opened the door and led him inside.

Max followed her, still talking. "I could figure out what

I'm doing, maybe. Get away from here for a few days, think about things."

"And be with me," said Mrs. Zeno.

"And be with you."

"Hurry, get what you need."

Max hurried. He put his thoughts on hold and simply moved. He did not dare look into Ben's room or Nora's as he went past. His suitcase was in the hall closet. He half filled it, and in a minute he was back downstairs.

"We'll have to go in your truck," Mrs. Zeno said.

"Fine, that's okay." Max's eyes were on the mantelpiece. The wedding picture, Nelly in white, smiling. The picture of Nora, Ben, and Bilko in the grass. He took them down, opened up his suitcase, and slipped them in.

"Are you ready?" said Mrs. Zeno.

"Almost." He went into the kitchen and stood at the counter writing a note.

Nelly, he wrote. *I love you. I am going away for a while. The world is so strange, and so sad. I love you. Forgive me. Max.* He put his pencil down for a moment, then picked it up again and wrote, *I'll be back*, and underlined these last words three times.

He looked up at Mrs. Zeno without smiling and said, "Let's go."

They ran for the pickup truck. Max put the suitcases in back and tied them down. Mrs. Zeno sat on the passenger side; he slid in behind the steering wheel. He held his door open and looked down at Bilko, who had followed them outside.

"Come on, Bilko, you want to come?" said Max.

She approached the pickup slowly, then stopped a few feet away.

"You want to come? Like always?" He thought of her jumping into the truck every day as he went off to do his lawns.

But she would not join him.

Max closed the door and turned to Mrs. Zeno. He was trying not to cry. "You promise they'll all be safe? You promise?"

"I promise."

Max started the engine and pulled away. He only went a few feet before the tears came. He turned on the windshield wipers, as if that would help in some way to clear his vision as he tried to see into the night.

As the truck picked up speed, Bilko started out after it. She ran and ran until the red taillights disappeared around a corner and were lost in the darkness.

Nelly drove up the opposite end of the street less than a minute later. She saw Bilko in her headlights, hurrying toward her, panting, tongue hanging way out. It was not a good sign, and it prepared her for what she did not see in the driveway, which was Max's pickup. When she got out of the car, she could smell exhaust from the truck still hanging in the air. She stood there, her heart beating rapidly, breathing it in, as if it were Max's scent and she could use it to track him down. But that, she knew, would not be possible. They could be headed anywhere.

Nelly knelt down and stroked Bilko's head. They looked at each other.

"I didn't make it in time, did I, girl? I don't suppose he told you where he was going? No? Well, you're not alone."

Nelly was trying very hard to keep it together. It had been one minute since she had discovered Max had left her, and she was doing pretty well. Now, if she could just make it through the next one.

She went into the house, took off her coat. She knew, from the feel of the place, that Ben and Nora were upstairs, blissfully asleep.

It would be in the kitchen, Max's favorite room. If he had left any word for her at all, it would be in the kitchen. As she went by the fireplace, an empty spot on the mantelpiece caught her eye. She stopped and fingered the dust that surrounded the area where the two pictures had been.

Ah, well, she thought. What did it mean? She put to her lips the trembling finger that had traced the dust. That he was not lost, she hoped. That he was still hanging on to his life with her.

She made her way into the kitchen, and there it was on the counter, the note. She picked it up, read it, put it down, then picked it up again.

"Max! Max! Max!" she cried suddenly, and ran out the back door. She reached her car, pulled open the door, and got in. She started the engine and was about to put it into gear, but she couldn't think which way to go. Forward? Backward? Which way had Max gone? Which way?

Nelly sat in the car for a time, slowly coming around. Now how many minutes have passed, she wondered, minutes without Max? There in the dark, she tried to think how many minutes there were in a lifetime.

For several hours Max drove without direction. He chose roads by their size, or because he felt like turning left for a while or he felt like turning right. Every so often Mrs. Zeno would reach over and touch him, and he would pull away. Gradually, he let her hand linger where it touched and allowed himself to look at her. The miles began to soothe him, her hand calm him, her look reassure him.

At last, in the early morning hours, she spoke. "Max, it is time to decide where to go."

With all Max's twistings and turnings, they had ended up only in Maryland, not a hundred miles from Gramenton. In the last miles Max pulled his pickup onto the roads that led south. Maybe it was instinctive—after all, fall was here, his season was over. He did not know where the birds wound up, to what special place they felt compelled to return. But he knew that the South was the only place that could satisfy his migratory urge.

"Peleg's Island," Max said, and eased the pickup off to the side of the road. He reached past Mrs. Zeno's lap into the glove compartment to find a map.

"Peleg's Island," repeated Mrs. Zeno. "Of course. What a good idea."

Max studied the map in the overhead light as he spoke. "Isn't it? It'll still be warm there, but hardly any tourists will be around, only the islanders. It's a great place to think."

"Yes," said Mrs. Zeno. "And the water will still be warm."

Max did not hear her. "Okay. I want to get to I-95. We're here just outside of Kingsley. We take 241 to 119, and then 119 over to east 62." He looked up. "About thirty-five miles to cut over to the interstate, and then it'll just be straight down from there."

Max felt better. Peleg's Island. He started the truck and headed for I-95. He'd be able to figure out some things when he got there. He needed to sit out on the pier, to walk on the beach. Images of water, sun, and sand lifted him, helped him hover safely above thoughts of home, thoughts of the beautiful woman sitting beside him—who was, unseen by Max, lifting her nose slightly and sniffing, trying to catch the smell of something that was still too far away to detect.

Nelly did not sleep in bed. She was not about to spend several hours in the place in which Max was most conspicuously absent. No, it was a night on the sofa, fully dressed. Bilko lay at her feet, each checking every so often to see if the other had fallen asleep.

"Well, Bilko," Nelly said at one point, "looks like we two old women weren't enough for him." She absently stroked Bilko's neck with her foot and thought about what Dr. Zeno had told her. Even with what he said, it was still hard to think of Mrs. Zeno as anything but the Other Woman. Nelly knew she had made a tactical error—she should have gone to Mrs.

Zeno first. And done what? Grabbed her hair and pulled her to the ground? Begged and pleaded?

But the biggest mistake of all was to have left Max alone. She should have stayed with him and held on until he came to his senses. Now look. Here she was alone on a sofa with no one to hold but a dog. Which is what she did. She moved to the other end of the sofa and wrapped her arms around Bilko, the first time she had ever done such a thing. They fell asleep that way, two abandoned women on the sofa.

Ben found them that way when he crept downstairs in the morning. He was creeping because he had gone to Mommy's and Daddy's room and had found an empty bed. That had never happened before, because he was always the first one up. He looked in the bathroom, and they were not there. So he crept downstairs because things were becoming too spooky. If they were not downstairs— Well, he did not even want to think about that.

"Mommy!" He caught sight of Nelly's arm draped over the back of the sofa in the living room. Both she and Bilko sat up at the same time, instantly awake. Ben jumped on Nelly, so relieved that it took him at least three seconds to realize that all was not completely right with the scene.

"Where's Daddy?" he said. "Why are you dressed already?" He was used to his mother padding around in her bathrobe in the morning.

The thing about children, Nelly knew, was that they always got right down to it. As muddled as her brain was, as barren of plans, she would have to come up with something. Obviously, it was not going to be, Your father has run off with another woman.

"Daddy's gone away," she began, the words like ashes in her mouth.

Ben looked puzzled, of course. "Away. To mow grass?" Too early, his face said. Does not compute.

"Well, not exactly." She stared at Ben and saw Max in his eyes. She had to turn from him.

"So where away?" Ben played with Bilko's ears, arranging them in different ways, and Bilko, in a rare generous mood, indulged him.

"On a trip, sweetie. On a business trip."

Ben brightened. He'd heard of business trips. His friends' fathers went on business trips. "Wow," he said. "That's great."

"It is," said Nelly. "Yes, it is."

"When's he coming back?"

Nelly winced. She'd forgotten about that question. "Oh, soon," she said softly. "You know. Soon."

His mouth opened for another question. Nelly didn't think she could bear any more. "What's for breakfast?" he said.

Later that day Nelly had three visitors. First, Billy in his mailman's uniform, who knocked gently on the front door then walked in.

"Hello? Anybody home?"

Nelly came slowly out of the kitchen. She shrugged and ran a hand through her hair. "One person, Billy. I'm sorry to report that only one person is home."

"Max?" Billy breathed.

"Gone."

"He took Ben and Nora?"

"No, no. Ben's at school. Nora's at day-care. I couldn't have her around."

Billy came across the room to her and took her hands.

"Gone where?"

"Where do you think? Away somewhere with Mrs. Zeno. That's her name, Mrs. Zeno."

They stood there holding hands, two of the saddest people in the world.

Billy stared into the eyes of the woman he loved. "What are we going to do? We've got to get him back."

"How, Billy? If I could get in a car and go after him, I would. Except I don't know where he went."

"Didn't he tell you anything? I mean, what happened here?"

She opened a drawer beneath the bookcase and brought out the note.

He read it. *I'll be back* was certainly hopeful. But what chilled Billy, what made his palms really sweat, were the words *The world is so strange, and so sad.*

"Tell me what happened," he said, looking up at her.

And she did.

Afterward, Billy paced the room. Max was right about the world. It was strange, sad.

"You see," said Nelly. "What can we do? Nothing. We don't know where he is. And it's not just that. Even if I found him, even if I dragged him home, which I would certainly try to do, it wouldn't be any good. He's got to want to come back to me on his own."

"He said he would." Billy picked up the note. "He promised. See how he underlined it?"

"Then that's what I've got, isn't it? A piece of paper with a promise on it."

By late morning Max and Mrs. Zeno had made it into Virginia. Already the dirt along the shoulders of I-95 had begun to change to red, sandy southern dirt. Max cracked the window, and the familiar old smell of pine filled the pickup.

"You have been driving a long while," said Mrs. Zeno. "It's my turn."

"You can drive a pickup?"

She laughed. "You have seen what I can do."

"Good point," said Max. He pulled over on the next span of wide shoulder. He stretched and walked up and down, touched his toes.

Mrs. Zeno watched as he did deep knee bends.

"Ridiculous?" said Max, smiling. "When I was little, my brother, Fred, and I used to think it was the funniest thing when my father did his stretches whenever he got out of the car. We'd jump around imitating him."

Max stood a minute looking out over a cornfield, the stalks dry and bent, the corn long since gathered.

"Those were happy times?" Mrs. Zeno said, coming around to face him.

"Yes, sure they were happy times."

She kissed him, a long, long kiss. Max closed his eyes and let himself be taken by her kiss, transported by it.

When she drew away, he slowly opened his eyes. "That was quite a—"

He stopped. The cornstalks were no longer dry and brown. They were young and green and about knee high. Knee high by Fourth of July, the sun throwing off the unmistakable southern heat of midsummer.

Max whirled around to where Mrs. Zeno had been standing. She was gone. The pickup was gone—and in its place stood the Lakeman family dependable, the 1964 Chevy station wagon. In the front seat sat Doris, in the prime of her young-mother years, staring through the windshield at Emmett going down for his twentieth and final deep knee bend.

Behind Emmett, a little boy with red hair and green T-shirt was doing wild jumping jacks and generally monkeying around. Fred.

"Hey look, Max. I'm Daddy!" Fred yelled over to him, and did push-ups in the red dirt.

Doris leaned out of her window. "You get up from there this instant, you hear me?"

Emmett poked at Fred with his foot. "Okay, wise guy, back in the car." He looked over at Max. "That goes for you, too, Bub."

Max's head went back and forth, from Emmett to Fred, to Doris fidgeting in the front seat of the Chevy. Then he looked down at himself. He was wearing a T-shirt, too, and blue shorts with an elastic waistband. His legs were short and hairless, there was a scab on his knee. Max fingered the scab in amazement. He hadn't had a scab on his knee in years.

"Come on, turkey brain, quit playing with yourself." Fred pulled him into the backseat of the station wagon.

"Hey, wrong side." Fred pushed him to the other side of the seat. "What's the matter with you, anyway? You know that's my side."

Max rode along, content. The car smelled so good, every move his mother or father made was a comfort to him, Fred's hot and bored stare at the whizzing landscape precisely as it should be.

In the corner of his vision Max saw Doris's fingers wiggling and scratching at the side of the front seat. The signal! Max eased down, keeping an eye on Emmett, and took hold of the candy his mother sneaked to him. Two Tootsie Rolls, the long skinny penny kind. Saint Doris ministering to the needy. The Tootsie Roll was sweet as a dream. He chewed it silently, the threat of being discovered by Emmett intensifying the sugary rush.

Max played rock-scissors-paper with Fred for a while, then he read old DC comics—Superman, the Green Lantern, and some *Mad* magazines.

Then Fred, operating on a schedule as predictable as the tides, said, "Dad? Daddy?"

Max knew what was coming. Doris, shifting in her seat, knew. And certainly Emmett, clenching the steering wheel even more tightly, knew. Knew and therefore did not answer.

"Daddy," Fred persisted.

"If you even say it," Emmett warned.

"But, Daddy."

"Don't you 'Daddy' me." Emmett tugged on his Phillies cap, as if trying to cover his ears.

"But I'm not the only one. Max has got to, too."

"I do not," Max piped in, his own little boy's voice surprising him.

"He does, he does. He's just too chicken to say so now." Fred shot a quick, triumphant leer at Max.

"This car was stopped twenty miles back, you guys had your chance then."

As always, as soon as Emmett held firm, the needle in Max's bladder tipped over to Full. Instant panic, as he scrunched his knees to his chest and prayed for mercy.

"Now, Emmett," said Doris.

"Oh, great, here we go," said Emmett, pounding the steering wheel. "I suppose you have to go now, too."

"Be reasonable, Emmett. It was not twenty miles, it was at least fifty, and besides, who cares how long it's been!"

"Jesus Christ."

"Daddy, hurry," whined Max.

"Hurry, Daddy, hurry," chimed in Fred.

"Emmett, you better hurry," pushed Doris.

Emmett jerked the steering wheel and the car braked in a spray of gravel. He turned his sweaty, exasperated face to his sons and growled, "I want you back in this car in thirty seconds. Got it?"

Max opened the door and scrambled out. He made it to a clump of bushes just over the guard rail. He unzipped himself and, not even surprised at what a tiny pink thing it was, relieved himself on the red Virginia soil. He closed his eyes gratefully, his spirits soaring as his bladder emptied. Then he zipped himself back up and turned.

To find no Fred, no Chevy with Emmett and Doris in it. But there was the pickup, the engine running, and Mrs. Zeno in the driver's seat. Max walked over to the truck and got in.

Mrs. Zeno kissed him. "Welcome back. You feel better?"

"Yes," said Max. "Much better." He moved his tongue around in his mouth and found a little clump of something stuck to his back molar. He rolled it around, savoring the sweet fading taste of Tootsie Roll.

* * *

Nelly's second visitor that afternoon was Clement. He did not so much visit as show up, pacing back and forth on the front sidewalk outside the house. After Billy went back to his mail route, Nelly sat down in front of an upstairs window simply to stare out, to do nothing and something at the same time. Thus she witnessed Clement's entire performance. And it was a relatively long one, full of hesitations, gestures in the air, facial contortions. First, his battered truck pulled up. He opened the door, got out, looked at the house, then got back in. Two cigarettes later he was out of the truck once again. It was another ten minutes before he made it from his truck to the sidewalk. Nelly could see him talking to himself, his mouth going, his arms moving up and down. Once on the sidewalk he started to pace, ten feet one way, ten feet the other. At last, with great effort and much fiddling with his cap, he started up the brick walk to the house.

He's got worms, Nelly thought. The worms of guilt and shame are crawling through his body, eating his bones, laying eggs in his belly. She did not let him get to the front porch. She banged on the second floor window, then opened it and looked down on him.

"You stop right there!" she called.

Clement did exactly as commanded, obedient to the angry voice from on high.

The expressions they wore, though Nelly's was tinged with anger and Clement's with remorse, were remarkably similar. Their unslept faces had a startled look, the look of having not yet digested an overgenerous serving of unsettling news.

Clement squirmed beneath Nelly's glare. "I got to see Max," he managed to get out. His neck was beginning to get a cramp from staring up at her. This made him squirm even more.

"Is that right," said Nelly. "You got to see Max?"

Clement wiped his nose on his sleeve and blinked.

Nelly went on. "What about, I wonder? You want to make sure I delivered your message?"

Clement flinched. "Please. I wasn't thinking."

"You weren't thinking. That's the goddamn understatement of the year." Nelly leaned out the window like she was about to jump on his back. "What are you doing here, anyway?"

"Please. I got to see Max."

"Stop saying 'please,' Clement. You don't know what words like that mean."

"I shouldn't have done what I did."

Nelly slammed the window shut. Clement could hear her running down the stairs. He wanted to run, too, but he stood there, braced himself as she flung open the front door.

"Get out of here, Clement!" Her face was red, her eyes fierce.

Whatever she did, he deserved. If she swung at him, he would not defend himself.

"No," he said, not moving.

Nelly's mouth opened wide enough for a scream, but no sound came out.

For a long moment neither of them moved or spoke.

At last Clement said, "What I did was wrong. It was none of my business."

"Why are you doing this?" Nelly tried to see into his eyes.

"And I'm sorry." With those words Clement could breathe again, could meet her stare.

"Why are you doing this?"

"Is Max here?"

"Why have you come? Why are you apologizing?"

Clement turned and looked over at the driveway. Max's pickup was not there. He hadn't noticed that before.

"Max is gone," he said, mostly to himself. Then he turned back to Nelly. "To work?" But he could feel her answer before she said the words.

"No. Gone," Nelly said in a whisper.

"I did this," said Clement when he could speak again.

Nelly had no more anger. She felt slow and calm. "You didn't do it, Clement. You just made things that were going to happen, happen a little faster, that's all."

"I don't believe you."

"Then believe what you want." She started to turn.

"Wait." He put his hand on her arm. They both looked at it, his big hand, black with old grease, on her pink skin. He drew it away.

"When Max comes home, I have to see him. I have to."

"When Max comes home," Nelly repeated.

"You won't forget?"

"When he comes home. Yes." She stepped inside the house and closed the door.

Clement went back to his truck and started the engine. When it didn't turn over the first time, or the second time, either, he didn't curse or slam his fist on the dashboard as he usually did. He waited patiently, then turned the key again. The engine coughed to life. Clement put the truck into forward and made his slow, careful way up the street. When he got to the corner, he turned right, then parked the truck beside a large forsythia bush. He adjusted the rearview mirror until he could just see the front of the Lakeman house, then lit a cigarette and waited.

Upstairs, Nelly sat once more at her window, her eyes set on a far distance. A scratching sound, at first not loud enough to pull her back. Again, scratching, and this time Nelly tilted her head. Now the scratching was furious, and she turned, just as Bilko pushed open the heavy door and hurried toward her. Bilko dropped something small and blue on Nelly's foot. Nelly bent down and picked it up. A sea shell. She held the shell in her hand as Max had once held it in his. And then she smiled at Bilko. Peleg's. Max had gone to Peleg's.

She turned toward the window as if she was about to call to him, to tell him to wait right there—don't move, I'm coming to get you. At that moment a car pulled up in front of the house, a purple convertible. Dr. Zeno got out, went around to the passenger's side, and opened the door. Then he looked up at the window and nodded to Nelly.

Meanwhile, just around the corner, Clement straightened in his seat, ready to move.

Max slept for a long time, and when he awoke, they were deep into North Carolina.

"Ummm," he said, running his hand through his hair. "I was really out."

"Good afternoon, my love," said Mrs. Zeno.

"Afternoon already?"

"You have been asleep for a million miles. Are you hungry? I stopped and bought us something."

Max took an apple and some cheese from the brown bag that sat between them. "Great. Good job."

"The people here speak so funny." She did a startling imitation of a variety of southern accents, the woman store clerk, the man who pumped gas while Max slept, a tollbooth attendant. "When they speak," she said, "it is as if they don't really want to let go of the words. It is all so slow."

"Everything is slower here." It was a good place to come. He needed to move slowly.

Mrs. Zeno pointed. "Those signs. Everywhere. 'South of the Border.' "

Max laughed. Mrs. Zeno was alert to everything, just as he was. "South of the Border is a place people think they want to go until they get there."

"You have been?"

"No. Not really."

"Why?"

"Because it's a place you only want to long for. It's no good actually getting there. The best part of South of the Border, when I was little, was all the signs."

"So many signs."

"Exactly. They start about two hundred miles away, and the closer you get, the more there are, the faster they come. But in the end, after all that expectation, it turns out to be nothing. It's nice to imagine, but not somewhere you really want to be. I'm glad now my father never let us get out of the car. Staying in the car kept it magic for me."

Ten miles later, when they drove past the tired Mexican hooplah of South of the Border, Mrs. Zeno turned her head back and forth taking it all in.

At a stoplight, a string of tourists passed before them, their faces expressionless. "It is not a very happy place," said Mrs. Zeno.

A bored father pulled on the hands of his two children, as his vacant-looking wife brought up the rear. "And the people are not happy, either," she said.

"They got out of the car. That was a big mistake," said Max, shaking his head. "The whole point is staying in your car."

They drove a few more miles, Max looking out at the old familiar things—the sandy fields, the tobacco barns leaning to one side, the little towns with white paint peeling off brick facades and Spanish moss hanging from telephone lines.

And though he didn't want to, he couldn't come this close without visiting Grandma Lakeman.

"Would you mind if we made a slight detour?" said Max.

"Anything, Max. You know that." Mrs. Zeno leaned over and kissed him when they came to a stop sign. She had taken on a southern scent. Her breath smelled faintly of wisteria, her hair of pine.

For the next twenty miles, Max talked about his grandmother. He told Mrs. Zeno how his grandmother would let down her hair and be the witch, how he and Fred would eat the figs and pecans that dropped from her trees, how he would walk around her cool clean house and stare at her dark and shining furniture. Max looked away from Mrs. Zeno as he spoke, for fear she would see in his eyes that the grandmother he described no longer existed.

They stopped in front of the white brick house, and Max sat quietly in his seat staring at it. He thought he saw Mrs. Winston's stolid black figure move past a window. Taking in medicine for Grandma? A bedpan? He didn't want to know.

"Let's go," he said, turning to Mrs. Zeno.

"But you wanted to come here."

"What I really wanted was to come to the place this used to be," Max said. "And if I don't get out of the truck and go in, I'll still have that. It's like South of the Border, I guess. If I go in, it will be Mrs. Winston and an old sick woman who doesn't know me. But if we keep going, it will be my grandmother in there fixing Bavarian cream pie for me and Fred."

Billy came speeding over to Nelly's on his red bike. He was still wearing his mailman's uniform. He had just finished work and gotten home when Nelly called. "Be right there," he said.

And he was. He turned into Nelly's driveway, out of breath, and stood his bike against the garage door. A giant man leaned on the purple convertible that was parked in front of the house. They stared at each other but did not speak.

"Billy. There you are." Nelly opened the front door. She was holding a wiggling Nora. Ben came up from behind Nelly and ran to Billy. They were old friends. Billy knelt down, and Ben took his mailman's cap, then ran back into the house.

"I'll handle things here," said Billy, taking Nora from Nelly. "Don't worry. Just go."

"Here are the house keys," she said, leaning close to kiss his cheek. Billy closed his eyes for moment.

"You going to be all right with that guy?" Billy jerked his head toward Dr. Zeno.

"I'm going to be all right." She kissed him again, then

ran across the lawn to the purple convertible. Dr. Zeno let her into the passenger's side, then went around the car and got in. He pushed a button and the white top slowly rose, covering them.

"Well," he said. "It is time to retrieve our wanderers."

The purple convertible pulled away from the curb and they were off, disappearing into the early evening light. Five seconds later and far enough back so he wouldn't be spotted, Clement sped along behind them. As he raced past the house, he stuck his arm out the window and waved to Billy. Billy returned his wave, and his uplifted hand stayed up, hanging stupidly in the air, as he realized who had just gone by.

And so Peleg's Island. Max and Mrs. Zeno drove the last twilight miles to the coast in silence. This time Max crossed the bridge to the island without Nelly, without Ben and Nora, without Bilko at his side. For a moment in the dark, he thought he crossed the bridge without Mrs. Zeno either. The seat beside him was empty. Then a hand reached from the shadows and came to rest on his leg, and he knew that she had not left him. Maybe, he thought as the first whiff of sea air reached him, I left her.

Now he could see Mrs. Zeno clearly as she rolled down the window and let the air blow over her. She was very excited. "Do you smell it, Max? Oh, it's wonderful. And I can hear the waves, Max!"

They drove to the end of the island, then down the sand driveway to the house. Max rested his hand briefly on the side of the house, an old friend, someone he knew, and who knew him.

"It's good here," he said.

"Yes," said Mrs. Zeno.

They opened all the windows, and the warm breeze filled the house. It was high tide, and in the moonlight the creek curved away from behind the house in a silver trail leading to the ocean. Max stood alone at the open window until Mrs.

Zeno came quietly beside him and took him by the hand and led him to bed. They made love, taking their rhythms from the waves and their sighs from the wind that blew in from the sea.

Afterward, when she was asleep, Max rose and went out to the back porch and lay down on the old army cot. It was the same cot he had slept in all those summers when he was a little boy—alone, in the dark with his glasses off. Max closed his eyes and heard voices coming from the house, voices from other times. He heard Doris, he heard Emmett answering, and Fred calling out for a glass of water from a farther room. Then the voices became soft and indistinct, and there were other sounds coming from along the far bank of the creek. Max went up on one elbow, as he had done so often as a boy, and looked out. He saw a point of light jiggling in the distance, then watched as it glided toward him. He heard hushed voices, low laughter, and the muted sound of oars pulling through the water. The boat, the boat was coming for him. He was asleep before it reached him.

Long into the night, and into the early hours of the next day, Clement followed Nelly and Dr. Zeno. Through Delaware, Maryland, Virginia, the Carolinas. At first it was difficult to keep them in sight, but as it got late, the traffic thinned. He never took his eyes off the large red rear lights of the convertible—red eyes that stared into his own, held him, so that he dared not look away.

Up ahead on the dark interstate, her head leaning back against the seat, Nelly stared, too. Her eyes were fixed on the road, taking in the curves, the signs, the dented guardrail. There was only this road, the road to Max. She did not speak to Dr. Zeno. She watched the road and listened to the wind blowing past the car, the engine straining against the miles, the wheels humming on the dark asphalt.

Dr. Zeno had said, in the only words they exchanged when she got in the car, "Nelly. We will go down to Peleg's

Island, but I must warn you I do not know what we will find there."

"Dr. Zeno," Nelly said, looking straight at him. "This is my chance. I didn't get a chance before. You just take me to him."

The purple convertible stopped twice for gas. Both times Clement had been sweating it out, watching his fuel gauge drop down to the red *E*. He pulled in to the unlit parts of the rest areas, then cut his engine. Nelly would get out and stand beside the big man, her hair tangled, her face white. She didn't speak to the man, only stretched a few times, went to the restroom, then got back in the car. When they pulled out, Clement sped over to the gas pumps. He handed the guy fifteen bucks, filled his tank, then got back in his truck and took off without waiting for his change.

Once, in Richmond, he pulled into an exact-change tollbooth and didn't have any quarters. He fumbled around for a minute, then drove on through without paying. Warning bells jangled behind him as he chased after the convertible. A sleepy attendant took in the scene, then roused himself and went out to shut off the alarm.

On and on they drove, the truck always somewhere behind the convertible. Daylight came, and the travelers squinted into the sun. The land around them had changed in the night. The dirt was red, the leafy fall trees of the north had given way to pine and scrub oak. They turned off the highway and headed for the South Carolina coast. It was warm now. Dr. Zeno put on a pair of sunglasses, and Nelly opened her window to let the air blow over her. Behind them, around a bend, Clement stared through the windshield at the foreign landscape and licked his lips and wondered where the road was taking him.

Max spent the morning out on the pier watching the creek and the marsh, as he had watched the night before. An egret walked carefully in the shallows. Two fish jumped, one behind the other. After a time he felt someone walking up the pier behind him. "Nelly," he almost said, turning, then shaded his eyes from the sun and saw that it was Mrs. Zeno.

"I'm going to the beach for a swim. Come along?"

"No. Thanks. Think I'll stay here for a while."

She leaned over and kissed him. "Are you sure? The water is beautiful."

"No. Not just yet. Maybe later. Okay?"

She left him. He watched her go until he could no longer see her white bathing suit.

He stared after her for a long while, then turned his gaze north, toward Nelly. Then, as if she was no farther away than the water flowing beneath his feet, he said, "I love you."

The words, the sound of his own voice, brought him to his feet. He began to move slowly up the pier toward the house, then faster. When he got to the stairs, he was running. Inside, in the bedroom, his suitcase lay open, its contents spilling onto the bed.

He began to pack, then stopped. There's no time. The only thing he took was the keys to the truck. He ran back through the house, his bare feet slapping against the wooden floor. He jumped in the truck, started it, and backed up the driveway, weaving from side to side. When he reached the road, the road that would take him off the island, over the bridge and northward, a breeze poured in the window, and he closed his eyes and breathed deeply and pushed his foot on the brake.

Max pulled back into the driveway and got out of the truck. He crossed the road and walked toward the beach. He did not feel the warm sand beneath his feet, or the sea oats brushing his arms as he crossed over the dunes. He stood on the last dune and looked out over the beach and, beyond it, to the water, dark green.

Mrs. Zeno stood at the water's edge. She waved. Then Max waved back. Their hands finally dropped to their sides and for a long time neither of them moved. Max lifted his nose to the breeze coming in off the water. He did not smell the salt or the sea air. He smelled grass, freshly cut grass. And when he looked out at the wide watery expanse stretching endlessly before him, he saw not the ocean, but a dazzling green lawn, and standing at its edge his beautiful woman in white.

Max walked slowly toward her as she opened her arms to him. Then, just as he reached her, he hesitated, and before he moved again, Mrs. Zeno stepped forward and wrapped herself around him. Two pelicans appeared above them and dropped pink flowers from their swollen bills.

"I love you," she said, her voice a sigh as soft as the petals that landed on their cheeks, their hair. Then she took his hand and gently pulled, led him into a sea of green.

Nelly and Dr. Zeno, turning at that moment into the driveway behind Max's truck, did not see the two figures moving slowly among the waves. Nelly ran past the truck toward the house, away from them, calling Max's name. She ran through the empty rooms, calling, her voice rising each time he didn't answer. She picked up one of Max's faded shirts, clutched it, and filled the air once more with his name. But the sound of her voice was too far away—it mingled with the wind and was lost among the cries of the birds.

It was Clement, Clement who had stopped his truck in an empty lot on the beach side of the road, who saw Max in the water. At first, leaning against the steering wheel, his head thick with fatigue, Clement squinted in the morning sun watching Nelly run down the driveway. He could hear her calling Max as she ran into the house. Then he turned his head the other way, toward the ocean he had not even realized was there. He could still hear Nelly, though faintly now. Her voice, he knew in an instant, would never reach Max. Max was in the water, moving rapidly away from the thin strip of beach.

The scene was wrong. Clement, shading his eyes, saw that Max was fully dressed. And he was not swimming, not swimming at all, but struggling, splashing helplessly in the water, the waves sucking at him. Sometimes he would go down then bob up again, his wet shirt sticking to his arms and back. Mrs. Zeno was farther out than Max and was turned away from him, swimming for the horizon.

Clement jumped out of the truck and ran across the dunes. "Hey!" he shouted. He was already out of breath and the beach seemed very wide and he was getting nowhere. Max was going down and staying down longer. Clement pulled at his clothes as he ran, throwing his shirt to the sand, kicking off his sneakers.

"Max, hold on. Hey, Max!"

Max had stopped struggling. He was floating, drifting away. A wave fell over him, then another, and Clement, in the water now, couldn't see him. Clement dove, the salt stinging his eyes. There was nothing, only dim bubbling green. He came up for air, treading water. Only Mrs. Zeno moved, her white suit shimmering in the distance. Max was nowhere. Clement dove again. When he came up once more, Max was floating on a wave, his arms out, his pale face turned up to the sky. The water moved, lifted Max's limp body high on a wave, and delivered it to Clement. Clement hugged Max close to him and did not let him go.

Nelly and Dr. Zeno were on the beach now, running into the shallow water. The three of them pulled Max onto the wet sand. Clement still clutched him. Dr. Zeno took Clement's arms and eased him away as Nelly dropped to her knees beside Max. She turned his head and bent down to press her lips to his, to push life into him. But Max made a small sound, another louder sound, then jerked his head, coughed up a bellyful of water, and breathed. Nelly cradled him, feeling him returning to her.

Clement watched Max until the coughing stopped, and the breaths came easier. Then he stood up, very shakily, and looked down at him. Max was trying to open his eyes. There was nothing Clement had to say to him now. He knew he had saved Max, had spared him, and would spare him again with silence. There were secrets to reveal, and secrets to keep, and Clement would always keep his. Nelly reached up and touched his hand. Clement held it a moment, then turned and walked away, gathering his clothes from the sand before disappearing among the dunes.

Max slowly opened his eyes, blinking in the sun. He knew the skin his head rested against, he knew the warm scent, he knew the voice that spoke his name.

"Max."

He smiled. He shifted and sat up a little, leaning on her.

Dr. Zeno stood before them, his great hands clasped in front of him, the wind lifting his silver curls. Behind him, a dot of white on a green ocean, Mrs. Zeno swam back and forth, waiting.

"Ah, well," sighed Dr. Zeno. "Husbands and wives. It is all so very complicated."

Nelly and Max moved closer together.

"It's time for us to go," Dr. Zeno said.

"Yes," Max said softly. Then he lifted his head so he would be heard. "It's time for you to go."

Dr. Zeno smiled at him, then turned and undressed himself, and swam in long, beautiful strokes toward his wife. For a time Max could see them moving in the sparkling water, then he couldn't see them anymore.

H·O·M·E·

*M*AX Lakeman, ever the family man, sat in his lawn chair in the thin shade of a dying peach tree. A year might not have passed since he last sat under the tree. After all, there was Nora playing beneath the picnic table, placing clumps of grass in a blue Dixie cup. There was Ben over beside the sandbox, trying to dress an unamused Bilko in a T-shirt. And there was Nelly, Nelly so beautiful, so radiant in the late-afternoon sun that Max caught his breath and stared. Calm down, Max, he told himself, all she's doing is setting the table for the barbecue.

But a year *had* passed. Max saw it in the peach tree, another branch going, its leaves curling, defeated in midsummer. He saw it in Nora and Ben, too. One year had brought words pouring out of Nora's mouth. She talked and talked. She spent her days pointing and urgently pronouncing words, then moving to the next thing, pointing, pronouncing, as if she was renaming all the world. Max heard her now, her tiny voice coming from beneath the picnic table. "Ketchup," she said. Then, "Relish."

Ben had long since renamed his world, and now in this past year had begun to venture out into it. Max, who had assumed that Saturday mornings with Ben would go on forever, found that his little buddy had moved on. Ben and two other neighborhood boys were in a club, and they had a secret place down by the creek behind the Cressons'.

"Daddy, I can't tell you," Ben frowned when Max had plied him for details. God, a club! Max began to drift. He remembered making official badges out of aluminum foil and ribbons, and saluting in some semifascist way and whispering the secret password, "Osiris-manachee."

"Can't you just tell me the name?" Max tried.

"That wrecks it, Daddy," said Ben, so seriously Max felt like the child who should have known better.

"It's not like I want to join, or anything," said Max, trying to recover his dignity. Alas, he did want to join, spend hours at the creek in deep adventure.

Ben had given him a look, a look Max knew in an instant he'd have to endure over and over in the father-son struggles ahead. It was the good-bye look. Good-bye, Daddy, I have to be moving along now.

"Well, anyway," Max had said, helping Ben into his boots, "have fun, and be careful."

"I won't go in over my boots, I won't play with broken glass, I won't cross Yale Avenue," Ben recited for his father, then wriggled away from him and was gone.

A year had passed, Max saw it in Bilko. Bilko never let Max out of her sight now. When he had returned from Peleg's, she had pushed open the front door and run across the lawn to him. Max had put out his hand, and Bilko, without sound or warning, bit it. Her message was clear. Max Lakeman, don't you ever, ever, do that again. She bit him, saw in his eyes that he understood the seriousness of his crime, then forgave him with a burst of long and joyous howls. Although she forgave him and was pretty sure he wouldn't do anything so stupid again, she still thought it wise to stick close. Close meant that Max could not go anywhere in a car or truck without her, even a three-minute drive for a quart of milk. Max would never again drive off without her.

Yes, Max knew, sitting in his lawn chair surrounded by his family, a year had passed. He saw it in talky Nora, in fearless Ben, in the white scar on the finger of his left hand, Bilko's reminder—and in Nelly. When Nelly turned her head as she bent over the barbecue grill, Max thought he could see the streak of gray that ran just behind her ear. A year ago it had not been there. Max had discovered it one evening in January. He was kissing the back of her neck, ascending toward her right ear when he suddenly stopped.

Nelly had murmured, "Don't stop." It had taken them a while to get used to one another again after Peleg's. There had been a period of undeclared chaste courtship from which they were slowly emerging. They were currently in a heavy kissing period.

"You've got gray hair," Max said.

"I'm not surprised," said Nelly. "Why don't you try kissing it away?" She nuzzled him.

"I'm not talking one or two hairs here. This is serious gray." His fingers searched her scalp. "This wasn't here before."

Before. They used a different calendar now. Before and after. Let's see, thought Nelly, what had the damage been? The physical damage was minimal. The gray hairs had been accumulating slowly—she first noticed them a week after they came home from Peleg's. Gray hairs, and a thin scar on the palm of her hand where she had grabbed the scalpel.

But there was greater damage, larger wounds, the extent of which only she would know. Max tried to know. He held her hand and kissed her head and tried very hard. But. But she had been the one left behind. Strange as the circumstances were, as powerless to the charms of Mrs. Zeno as Max may have been, he did the leaving, and she was the one left. He would never know that desperation.

The never-know factor. Nelly once had a patient with a

great wound in his belly. He'd been in the hospital for months, but the thing would not heal. Nelly made a mistake one day and said, out of helpless kindness, "I know it hurts, Mr. Torrey. I know just how you feel."

"Little girl," Mr. Torrey had said. He was ninety-four and called, rightly, all the nurses "little girl." Even Nelly didn't mind. "Little girl, I'm sorry, but you're wrong. Unless you ever have a wound like mine, you will never know, *never know*, how I feel."

Nelly had a wound. At first it had been a big wound, like Mr. Torrey's. But she was luckier than Mr. Torrey because she was going to heal. Nelly was both the nurse and the patient, hurting, but knowing, too, it was essential to work past the hurt. The first thing she did in the days that followed Peleg's was tell Max that she forgave him. Those words, like an ointment or antibiotic, were the essential cure. Nelly applied those words to the wound and slowly, imperceptibly, the healing began. Over the days and months they returned to one another, moving softly, carefully, and with the tenderest regard.

When they could talk about it, late in the winter months, Nelly asked, trying to sound casual, "So, um, Max, how was she?" Common sense, of which she had endless amounts, said don't do it. Don't ask, she told herself, but she was curious —how desirable could a woman possibly be? What, in fact, had she been competing against?

Max pretended not to hear. He shifted in bed. He hid his head under his pillow.

"Come on, Max. How was she? I'm just curious, that's all. I'm not going to get mad. I know she must have been pretty good at least." She poked him until he came out from under the pillow.

"Jesus, Nelly," he said. "Of all the things to ask."

"Tell me."

"Tell you what?"

"You know, details, what you two, you know . . ."

"Did?"

"Did."

Max sat up in bed and put his arms behind his head. He looked at Nelly and was silent for a moment. They had reached another great watershed in the healing process. The wife exorcising the sexual threat of the other woman. Max thought about the white room and the pallet, the naked perfection of Mrs. Zeno. Is this what Nelly really wants to know? And if she does, am I, in a million years, ever going to tell her? Nope. Not a chance.

"Well," said Max, scrunching his eyes a little, as if in soul searching concentration, "the truth is, this sounds weird, I know. But the truth is, sex with Mrs. Zeno was a little disappointing."

"Oh, come on," said Nelly. There was a trace, just a trace of a smile at the corners of her mouth. "I know she could do some pretty amazing things."

"Yeah, sure, I guess," said Max. "She could do things, and I suppose that's what confused me, made me think that more was there than, in fact, there actually was. She was pretty good, but not really that good."

Nelly was trying not to smile. "Keep talking, you're doing all right."

"There's nothing to say," Max shrugged, the dryness leaving his mouth as the marital road ahead cleared. "I don't think about that part of it much, believe it or not. It's hard to feel connected to a woman who did not"—he paused and licked his lips, almost tasting the salty ocean—"who did not have my best interests at heart."

Nelly slid across the bed to him. "I'll say."

Max had lied to Nelly. He did remember Mrs. Zeno and every moment in the white room, and what they did there was never a disappointment. But he could not think of those times without tasting salt water. When he thought of the white room, another image soon came to him—water everywhere and Mrs. Zeno's white figure pulling away, leaving him to struggle in the waves. It was an image that made you appreciate that ordinary, day-in–day-out being, your wife. Goodness, how Max appreciated Nelly.

Max remained a man of two worlds, this one and that one. But he chose, in the end, to live in this one, the one right here, the one he could appreciate from his lawn chair, the world of his small life, his own backyard, Bilko, Ben and Nora, Nelly standing beside the grill. That one, the world elsewhere, of the Zenos and wondrous odd things, was a terrain he was increasingly less likely to travel. Still, it would always be with him, sparkling in the far corners of his vision.

There was a sparkling now, flames dancing. Nelly had put a match to the grill.

"Here come Billy and Annie," she called to him.

The two of them came whizzing down the driveway on their bikes. Annie was the new girl friend. Actually she was Billy's old girl friend. She had left the guy in Cincinnati for good, had come back to Billy. Billy had never had a woman come back to him before. It felt pretty nice.

Billy put his knapsack full of beers on the bench, then went over to Nelly and kissed her on the cheek. He could do that now without breaking into a sweat. Nelly was no longer the woman of his dreams. He was exceedingly grateful that he had never opened his mouth about it or made some ridiculous overture. Time had straightened him out, time and the reappearance of Annie.

"Here," Billy said, tossing a beer to Max. "Let's do it."

They both took long, ungraceful swigs, then moved side by side, lifted their heads, and released, simultaneously, a duet of protracted burps. It was a stunt they had spent the summer perfecting.

Annie looked at Nelly. "Such children. I don't know why we bother."

Max said to Billy, "I think our dates are impressed."

"Oh, I know they are," said Billy.

"Some guys got it, . . ." Max chanted.

"And some guys don't!"

They laughed, happy to be together, the glow of the first late-afternoon summer beer easing through them. The lawn chairs beckoned, and they wandered over to them, leaving the smoking grill and the women.

"Will you look at them," said Billy dreamily.

"Life is good," said Max.

"Time to make a good thing better, I'd say." Billy took a gulp of beer and squirmed a little.

"Is it, now?"

"Well, it turns out that Nelly is not the only great woman in this world."

"I had a feeling that was probably true," said Max.

"I'm starting to have big thoughts about Annie."

"Big thoughts with a capital *B*?"

"Yeah, well, what the hell."

"Wow."

"From what I've seen, any fool can get married."

"Apparently," Max said.

Then they both smiled.

A station wagon hurtled into the driveway, spraying gravel. The other guests had arrived, Emmett and Doris. Emmett honked, two shorts and a long, then got out and opened the door for Doris. She emerged shakily, smoothing bits of discomposed hair. Obviously, the drive over had been a bad one. Knowing he was late, Emmett had probably gotten the car airborne. Poor Doris's arms looked rigid from bracing herself against the dashboard.

"We're here!" she called out gamely.

"We're late!" Emmett said, plunking a great bowl of potato salad on the picnic table.

"Dad, it's okay. You're retired now, late doesn't matter," Max said.

"A lot you know," gruffed Emmett. "Hello there, Billy. Annie, hello."

"Hello, Emmett," said Billy. "We only just got here, too."

"That means you're late, too," said unrelenting Emmett.

"Oh, Emmett," said Doris.

"Just making an observation," he said. "I could use a beer. Ben. Go get your old grandfather a beer."

"Kiss your grandmother first," said Doris, holding out her arms.

"That poor child's going to be kissed out by the time he's ten," said Emmett.

"Dad, you want to sit?" Max pulled the lawn chairs closer to the picnic table.

"No. I'm all right." Bilko moved out of his way as he paced the lawn. "Hello there, Bilko, you still alive?" The two of them had never been close. She ignored him and went over to sit beside Max.

Doris the love machine found Nora. Nora gave her the attention she craved for exactly two minutes, then ran away to the sandbox. Nora was too busy to ever spend more than two minutes on any one thing.

Max waited in his chair for the coming inspection. Doris sidled over to him while the others were talking. She squinted at Max like she was looking through a microscope.

"See anything?" Max finally said.

"I see you don't eat enough. You look five pounds thinner than last year."

"And last year I looked five pounds thinner than the year before. In another ten years I should be small enough to fit in your pocketbook."

"Smart," she said. "Like your father."

"Come here," Max said, pulling on her arm. "This is a two-way street." He perused the side of her neck. The mole —it was gone!

"Something the matter?" said Doris demurely.

"Where is it?"

"Where's what?"

"Your m-o-l-e."

She smiled. "So you finally noticed. I had it removed four weeks ago. So there."

Doris was very pleased with herself. Removing the mole was part of a little beautification program she'd recently begun. Looking good for my man. That's what the women's magazines were calling husbands these days—"your man." Emmett was the man in her life, and she was determined to look good for him. She followed the "Tips for the Older Woman" and fiddled with her hair, tried just a hint of Misty Moon eye shadow, soaked her hands in lotion when Emmett wasn't around. Henry Conaway, walking his beagle, noticed her efforts right off the bat.

"My, you're looking special today, Doris," Henry had said last week.

"Well, I'm not looking special for you!" she retorted, taking her charms back indoors where they were safe.

Emmett, though he was slower on the draw than Henry, finally acknowledged, in his own way, that something about Doris was different.

"What's wrong with your hair?" he said.

That had gotten him a full afternoon of the silent treatment. By dinnertime he had wised up.

"Aw, come on, Doris," he said, putting his arms around her as she stood stiffly in front of the stove.

"Don't bother," she whispered, her voice trembling.

"I like your hair this way, I do. And your eyes, don't think I didn't notice." In fact, he hadn't noticed until hugging her just now. A lucky break.

She made a small, noncommittal noise.

He went on. "You know me, Doris. I'm just not very good at this stuff. And besides, I don't want you to feel you have to do yourself up for me."

She turned. "I know I don't have to. I just want to because
. . . because you're my man." She blushed.

Her man? What in God's name had she been reading?
But Emmett was touched. Poor sweet Doris, he thought, how
could I ever have thought of leaving you? There was not a
woman on this earth besides Doris who could think of me,
pop-eyed, a mouth full of dentures, hairless, old, and grouchy,
as her man.

Emmett had gazed into her eyes, eyes a little watery from
overapplication of Misty Moon, kissed her, and said, "Doris,
I am your man, and you are my woman."

Annie clapped her hands and called out into the backyard,
"Let the hordes assemble, the feast is about to begin."

Bilko assembled first and tried to get up on the table, the
temptation of a plateful of unprotected hamburgers proving
too great. Max caught her before her jaws clamped down on
a patty.

He lowered her to the ground and said for all to hear,
"Oh, treacherous beast, oh, conniving canine, how could
you!" Then he whispered, "Stick with me, kid, I'll slip you
something later."

Emmett, wearing his Phillies cap and sitting at the head
of the table, waited for Ben to serve him. Ben liked to pretend Emmett was the King. Emmett would say, "The King
wants two hamburgers!" and Ben would ceremoniously deliver them to him. "The King wants ketchup!" Emmett
wasn't even allowed to squirt the ketchup on his hamburgers;
Ben had to do everything. The game ended when Ben
slipped and dumped half a jar of olives onto the King's lap.
He was about to burst into tears, but the King gave him a
royal pardon.

They sat at the table for a long time. They told jokes,
ate potato salad and hot dogs, played tricks, spilled cups of
soda and bottles of beer; Nora laughed and Ben cried; then
Nora cried and Ben laughed. Bilko slunk between hairy legs

and short legs and feet that were wearing sandals and white socks, snuffling up pieces of hamburger bun and bits of ice cream cone.

Afternoon became evening, and now the family was scattered around the backyard. Emmett and Doris sat in lawn chairs, holding hands in the dark. Billy lay in the grass, his head resting on Annie's stomach. Nora was asleep on a blanket. Nelly and Max lay on their backs in the grass, looking up at the stars. Only Ben moved. He was catching fireflies.

"Eight, Grandpa. I got eight now."

"Okay," said Emmett. "Two more to go."

Max turned his head so his cheek rested in the grass. He saw Bilko on her back, kicking her legs toward the stars, wallowing. That's what he wanted to do, wallow in the grass. In the winter, when he'd been healing, he would come out into the backyard and stare at the frozen ground. Then, the grass was brown and sparse. He and the world were dormant. But he knew that if he was patient and quiet, if he just waited out the days and months, the seasons would change. Spring would come again. Spring, and then the tiny pale shoots would push through the dirt and turn green in the glorious sun. The green did come, and he had been ready. His mowers were clean and rested, and he walked once again under the trees and across the lawns.

Max picked a single blade of grass and brought it to his lips. For a moment he was transported by its taste, its feel. At the edge of his vision lay a sparkling world.

The fireflies. Ben brought his cupped hands close to his father's face.

"See, Dad, ten. I caught ten now."

Emmett rose and joined the boy. "All right now, easy." They placed their hands together and Emmett took some of the insects from him. Max watched as his son and his father peered into their cupped hands. The glow lit their faces, shining from without and, Max knew, from within. When Emmett and Ben released the shimmering insects, Max still watched their faces, because the glow remained.

Emmett said, "It's getting late."

"Awww." Ben knew what that meant.

Doris gathered up her bowl and the bag of tomatoes Max had picked for her. "Give Grandma a kiss," she said to Ben. Ben ran away in a pout. Kissing her meant the party was over. Max knew that pout would be followed by sudden acceleration, then instant collapse. He figured Ben was good for about fifteen more minutes of consciousness.

Max walked Doris and Emmett to their car. Doris got in, and Emmett and Max stood a minute in the dark.

"You know, it's all been pretty good, hasn't it?" said Emmett softly.

"It has," Max agreed. "I wonder why?"

Emmett was silent. Then he said, "No reason that I can think of."

Max stepped back as Emmett started up the Chevy. Doris turned and waved, and Max waved back, his hand still moving long after the station wagon had vanished into the night.

Billy and Max sat beneath the stars while Annie and Nelly put the children to bed.

"So," said Billy.

"So," Max said back at him. He knew what was coming.

"So, how are you doing?"

Billy liked to check up on him every now and again. He never asked for details.

"Fine, Billy. All clear."

"You'll keep me posted, right?"

"Sure," said Max. "You'll be the first to know." He smiled in the dark.

The two friends shared a last beer, and then the women came out to join them. No one spoke until Billy finally groaned and rose. Annie stood at his side.

"The time has come for all good things to end," said Billy.

Nelly and Max watched as they got on their bikes. Billy started to pedal down the driveway, Annie ahead of him, and then he suddenly stopped and turned to look one last time at his two old friends, standing side by side in the summer dark. After a moment he started off again, honked his horn twice, and disappeared.

Nelly hugged Max. "Would you like to come to bed with me?"

Max closed his eyes and pushed his nose into her hair. "I want nothing more than to come to bed with you." Then he took a look over her shoulder. "Just let me take care of the dog first." Bilko sat a few feet away, waiting.

"Will I ever come before Bilko, do you think?"

"Do you want me to lie to you?"

Nelly raised an eyebrow at Bilko. "You've got five minutes with my husband, then he's mine for the rest of the night. Got it?"

Together, Max and Bilko enjoyed the last moments of a summer night, wandering around in the backyard, the grass warm beneath their feet. They paused beside the picnic table as Bilko briefly sniffed for remains of the barbecue, then they made their way across the lawn to the dying peach tree. Max leaned against it, listening in the dark. Heat lightning lit a distant corner of the night sky. It was very quiet. Max licked his lips and swallowed when something moved down at the far end of the yard where the rhododendrons grew. Bilko looked at Max. Max looked at Bilko. They both looked at the rhododendrons. Again, something big rustled leaves and shook branches. Max held his breath. Bilko stood motionless.

And then a white figure slowly emerged.

"Oh, my God, Bilko," said Max.

Bilko stiffened, and in one terrible moment the Pinkleys' trespassing Dalmatian realized she had been caught again.

"Bilko, go get that villain dog," Max shouted. "You're the only one who can keep this world safe!"

Bilko charged down the backyard, barking and barking, determined to keep Max safe forever.